9/09

D0955589

Sophia and the Seven Goddesses

Sophia and the Seven Goddesses
A Journey to Self-Acceptance

www.sophiadolls.com

Dedication

To the millions of women and girls who look in the mirror every day and do not feel like they measure up to the ideal beauty defined by the world. And, to my husband George who made my dream come true.

Acknowledgements

These acknowledgements are not just for the people who have helped support the writing of this book, but also for the many souls who helped give birth to the products that brought about the need for this amazing book. From the deepest place in my heart, I want to express my love and gratitude to everyone who has supported me.

"*Sophia and the Seven Goddesses: A Journey to Self-Acceptance*" is a result of many hearts collaborating to bring forth a vehicle that would support women and girls around the world to awaken to their Sophia, their wisdom.

As I acknowledge each person, please note that I am not putting names in order of importance, rather, on a timeline, with the exception of my loving husband, of when these beautiful people came to assist me in my mission. From the deepest place in my heart, I express my love and gratitude to everyone who has loved and supported me in the birth of my mission to empower women and girls through claiming and using their wisdom.

I am indebted to the thousands of women who have attended my workshops, retreats, and presentations, and who have intimately shared with me their fears and concerns of self-love and self-acceptance. Without you, Nea Matia, Inc., home of SophiaDolls™, would not have been possible.

My deepest gratitude goes to my precious soul mate and best friend, George Danusis, for funding the SophiaDoll projects, including this book. I thank him for being my "Greek God" who empowered me to never give up on my mission, even when I argued that I should. He continues to provide a lovely and safe haven for me, so that I can do my heart's work of empowering women and girls. I also want to thank him for his creativity, which he gave so freely to the book.

To my daughter, Beth Walter, a beautiful and talented teacher, for being my best girl friend and biggest fan, and for sharing my dream of empowering women and girls, I am forever grateful. I thank her for her tenacious support with each new idea and concept that I have ever come up with, which have been many. Her edits to this book have made it even more "tween friendly," and her love for children has been my greatest asset to the SophiaDolls projects.

To my son, Nathan Walter, a gifted composer and singer, and father of my two priceless grandsons, Stefan and Nicholas, a thank you for his encouragement and all he has taught me about wisdom and understanding.

My appreciation goes to my mother, Ruth Dail, and stepfather, David Dail, who believed in my ability and me to bring forth these products.

To the adorable Goddess CJ McGyver, the very best assistant anyone could have, I give deep thanks for her skill, witty humor, and wonderful personality that kept me going when things were tough in the beginning of creating the SophiaDolls and workshops.

My warmest appreciation goes to my dear friend, Bill Turrentine, who never stopped believing in my dream or me, and whose critical and artistic eye helped bring about the refined shape of the dolls.

To each of my loving spiritual teachers, who along the way held me in the Light and encouraged my mission as I endeavored to empower women and girls through the power of Wisdom/Sophia, I give my most heartfelt love and respect.

I am ever so grateful to Donn Chappellet of Chappellet Wines who believed in SophiaDolls so much that he gave the seed capital to do the necessary research and prototypes for our dolls. Donn has been blessed with many goddesses in his family: three beautiful daughters, his creative wife, Molly, his precious mother, Pat, and his caring sister, Sybil, not to mention his darling granddaughters. Of all men, he undoubtedly understands and values the feminine wisdom.

My most sincere appreciation goes to my soul sister, Chris Love, the enormously talented sculptor and artist of SophiaDolls and its projects, and to Devon, her remarkably talented husband for his clever contributions. Her excellent "eye" for color and form shows up in each doll she has molded in clay. This goddess of a woman has been with me nine of the ten years it took me to develop and manufacture SophiaDolls.

I offer my most sincere gratitude and thanks to Tony Genadio, who taught me the doll manufacturing business. When "they" said such a doll could not be made because it had never been done before, Tony said, he could do it and, indeed, he did.

A thousand thanks to my brilliantly gifted goddess sister, Diane

vii

Estrada, for her stunning abilities, relentless support, and love, and for standing by my side, like the Goddess Athena. She has gone to battle and fought many dragons with me. Her intelligence and resourcefulness has shown throughout Nea Matia, Inc. as she has woven her dream with mine to empower women and girls.

To my intelligent and beautiful step daughter, Chris Thiel, I am thankful for her never-ending belief that SophiaDolls would be manufactured, regardless of how bleak times became. To my son-in-law, Joe Thiel, who worked hard to market the dolls, I thank him for his tireless efforts. And to my grandsons, Wyatt and Zander, who have always believed in Sophia, a big thank you from Nonna's heart.

A very special thanks to my dear friends, Sue and Mike Kline, who would have invested everything they had to see that this project was completed. Their smiles and encouraging words were powerful food for my soul.

To my granddaughter, Mighty Mac, and my niece, Kaitlin, who played with and tested the dolls for me, thank you for providing me with a much needed young girl's perspective, which is so necessary to keeping my mission authentic.

I wish to thank another goddess-sister, Ilene Satala, the author of *Sophia and the Seven Goddesses,* who is an awe-inspiring story-teller and artist. She took the concepts and ideas of the SophiaDolls' team and combined them with her own genius, and wrote a story that all will love to read. She, too, has a mission to empower women and girls to use their feminine wisdom. I will always be indebted to her for sharing her beauty and wisdom with me. She is a true "SophiaWoman!"

I would like to acknowledge the main editor, Sherry Folb, for her commitment to excellence and for being the best editor anyone could ask for. Sherry worked many, many hours with Ilene and me making sure every word, sentence, paragraph, and concept was clear and perfectly written for the benefit of empowering women and girls.

Ilene Satala wishes to thank her husband and true-life companion, Conrad, who is the greatest light in her life, for always bringing her to wisdom's threshold, and for his inspiration and wise contributions to the book. She would also like to thank Joy Heinbaugh for her encouragement in the writing of this book, as well as her sister Darlene who was the recipient of many of Ilene's stories and who always asked for more.

Contents

Introduction

One day during a self-esteem workshop, which I was facilitating, a woman commented to the class that she strongly felt that certain types of dolls had a lot to do with how women grow up feeling about their bodies. I began researching the matter and learned that she was right. Studies have proven that dolls like Barbie and Bratz have negatively influenced young girls because the dolls act as role models. Reports also stated that 95% of women today do not honor or even like their bodies because they try to conform to the "ideal beauty" standards set by media for the fashion and toy industries.

I then read an article that quoted Dr. Joan Lester, Director of Counseling and Psychological Services at Saint Joseph College, who said, "In America, we're obsessed with how we look. Studies have found that by the 5th grade, girls are already beginning to diet, have already looked at themselves in the mirror and thought, 'I am fat.'"

As I fought my own inner battles and watched my daughter struggle with her issues involving body image, I knew I had to do something. I wanted to create a fresh message for women and girls about beauty and self-esteem. I also wanted to expand the definition of beauty—since beauty was too narrowly defined.

The direction was simple—develop a product that more accurately reflects who young girls are and allows them to make peace with how they look. Then came the inspiration to create dolls with more honest and realistic body proportions, model them after the ancient Greek goddesses and their attributes—and tie each doll to a special power that could be recognized, learned, and utilized.

My hope is that these dolls and their accompanying adventure books, which include a parent guide, will send a new and healthier message to counteract the growing number of products and images that young girls are faced with everyday.

My mission became: To educate, inspire, and empower all women, especially girls and their mothers, by providing fun educational products and experiences that combine playing and learning. This hopefully would facilitate the development of skills that supported an easier transition into and through teen years. My goal was to create a needed paradigm shift where we could trade the old fantasy of the "ideal beauty" to a more "wholesome and authentic beauty."

The pain of not measuring up to an imposed ideal has touched almost every family at some time or another. SophiaDolls™ provide a way to teach and empower girls and women how to be happy with who they are and how to discover the "genuine beauty" that lies within them.

I encourage you to read *Sophia and the Seven Goddesses: A Journey to Self-Acceptance* with your daughter, granddaughter, surrogate daughter, niece, or friend and share Sophie's adventure of self-discovery, self-love, and self-acceptance.

When you've finished, spend some time playing and doing the exercises at the back of the book. Who knows what you both might discover. Please write to me. I would love to hear your thoughts concerning my mission.

Lovingly,

Beverley Danusis, CCO and Founder of SophiaDolls Nea Matia, Inc.

P.S. As an added attraction, I've used a little dove to indicate the major messages in the book.

Chapter 1

Summer Vacation Begins

The sky was a deep blue with white clouds stacked like cotton candy as Sophie walked outside. She took a deep breath and thought, "It is a perfect day." This was the last day of school and the first day of summer vacation.

School was okay; Sophie loved to learn and was curious about everything. She was always reading about things she wanted to know more about. But summer vacation was all about having time to herself. She could do as much or as little as she wanted. So, for Sophie, this feeling of being free was simply the best feeling ever.

Kids flew past as they ran to the right and left of her. Everyone was excited about starting their first day of vacation, too. She waved and smiled at those she knew. "Have fun!" she yelled.

Sophie turned and headed for home. She loved to walk home, especially at this time of year. Winter was finally gone, which meant the flowers were blooming and the grass was changing from brown to bright green.

Chapter 1

She gleefully pulled her purple cell phone out of her pocket. How it sparkled in the bright sunlight—thanks to all the rhinestones she had decorated it with. It was growing warm in her hand as she prepared to give it a workout.

Quickly and with experienced ease Sophie entered text into her phone. "Hi, every1" she wrote. "I have a ? 4 U. What's UR favorite thing to do during the summer?" She hit the send button and now all of her best girlfriends would instantly be receiving her question on their own cell phones.

Texting was so much fun, and soon answers would be pouring in from the eight girls whose names and phone numbers she had on her favorite's list. She walked on along the familiar route, waiting for her friends' responses.

As she passed through the outer edges of her neighborhood, she realized that she knew the names of just about everyone's dogs, and a goodly number of cats, between here and her house. She knew the mailman's name and quite a few of the older neighbors who liked to work in their yards.

The truth was that Sophie loved people. And she had never met a dog or a cat that she did not like. Since she had no brothers or sisters, she had actually found talking to adults interesting.

Sophie's parents were both professors and her grandparents were, too. Her parents regularly had people over to the house who led fascinating lives and who were willing to sit down with a twelve-year-old girl and tell her stories of their adventures or their new ideas.

Sophie glanced at her phone and saw that it was loading up with messages. "Fantastic," she thought, "this is going to be such fun."

First, there was Jena. She wrote that her favorite thing to do on summer vacation was to ride her bike in the park. Sophie could picture Jena's bike with its silver trim and sky blue seat. Jena sat tall and gracefully on her bike.

In contrast, Sophie liked to hunch forward on her bike and peddle fast, racing across the park. When she reached the right speed, she would take both hands off the handlebars, raise both arms straight out to the left and right of her body, and pretend to fly. It was such a terrific feeling.

Sophie clicked the next message on her phone. It was from Faith. Faith wrote that she loved eating popsicles—especially cherry ones on an exceptionally hot day.

Now everyone reading this text message would remember last summer when the girls were all together and someone had suggested having a popsicle eating contest. Everyone ate their popsicles with loud slurps. Then, Faith had stuck her tongue out. It was very bright red.

Suddenly, they were all doing it, comparing who had the brightest, reddest tongue. The popsicles started melting and dripping and the giggling started. And so it went, until the popsicles were gone, and everyone had red tongues, lips, and fingers.

"Good 1," Sophie wrote back.

Kaitlin typed that during summer vacation she loved going to the amusement park and screaming as loud as she could on the roller coasters. The amusement park was quite a distance from home—it took nearly two hours to get there. The girls were lucky because their parents took turns taking all of them to the amusement park at least once during the summer.

Last year it had been Sophie's father's turn to take them. She actually had felt sorry for him because the girls kept running him around the park and screaming on the roller coasters until they were so hoarse they couldn't scream any more. The next day when her dad slept late, Sophie realized that they had worn him out. She texted back to Kaitlin, "We gotta do it again."

Another message clicked in and Sophie read how Mackenzie loved sleepovers and staying up late. It was the staying up late part that was the best in the summertime. Mackenzie's father would usually come downstairs to the family room where all the girls camped out. The room would be adrift in yellow, lavender, and pink sleeping bags.

He looked tired and in his most serious voice would announce, "Okay, girls it's time to go to sleep, don't ya think?" Everyone would grow quiet and jump into their sleeping bag.

But once he had gone back upstairs, someone always started to whisper, which led to someone giggling, and then everyone would be whispering and giggling again.

"We're all supposed to be sleeping," Mackenzie warned. That meant everyone just giggled harder. The more they tried to stop giggling and keep quiet, so that Mackenzie's father could get some sleep, the more they giggled—until they were totally out of control.

Sophie giggled out loud and wrote back, "Let's do it soon. At UR house, Mac?"

Chapter 1

As she walked along, she realized she was still giggling just thinking about it. They had such good times together. As she slowly read her text messages, she found herself thinking about all the fun she was going to have with her friends this summer.

She thought how they were all connected to each other through memories and laughter and adventures. Then, she experienced the strangest feeling. She could not remember ever having noticed anything like this before. It was this feeling at the center of her chest. She felt all soft, warm, and tingly.

It was a good feeling. How could she describe it?

She felt peaceful, happy, and warm. Not warm from the outside, but warm from the inside. It was as if she could feel the smiles of all her friends pouring through her. It was a good feeling to have on the first day of summer vacation.

Chapter 2
The Surprise

All of a sudden, the phone in Sophie's hand rang and caller ID read MOM. She answered, "Hi, Mom."

"Where are you, Sophie?" her mother asked. "I thought you would have been home twenty minutes ago."

"Oh," Sophie said, "I'm just enjoying walking and taking my time. It's so pretty today."

"Well," her mom said, "I have a surprise for you, dear."

"What is it?" Sophie asked.

Her mom laughed, "Well, honey, it wouldn't be a surprise if I told you, would it?"

Sophie laughed and called out with excitement, "I'll be home in a flash." Sophie's mother was of American-Indian descent, and she could picture her mom's long black hair and dark eyes. Her mother's heritage was Navajo and Sophie had heard many stories of her grandmother who was a fine weaver and wise woman. Her colorful rugs hung in their house and told beautiful stories.

Chapter 2

Sophie saved her text messages and sent out one final message to her friends. "G2G. Will e-mail L8R. Have to get home. A surprise is w8ng 4 me. Hope it's COOL." Sophie sent the message and began to run home.

By now she was only a few blocks from her house. As her short legs picked up speed, she rounded the final block and skidded toward the door, grabbed at the iron railing, and swung herself up the three steps to her back door. Sophie bounded through the kitchen, pulled off her backpack, and grabbed a cookie from a plate sitting on the kitchen table, all in one swift motion.

A few more steps and she ran into the living room, chewing on her cookie. "Mom," she announced, "I'm home." Then, she looked around the living room. To her surprise, sitting on the dark brown leather couch she saw her dad's parents, her grandmother, Beth, and her grandfather, Dimitri.

She could not help it. She let out a yell of delight and ran toward them. They stood up to hug her and pure joy filled the room. "Oh, how wonderful!" Sophie shouted. "You're back! You're back!"

Sophie hugged them both, her arms stretching out and pulling them both toward her. "I really missed you Gia Gia and Pa Pou." By now both grandparents were hugging her back and were laughing happily. It truly was wonderful to see one another again after being apart for two years.

"Sophie, Sophie," her grandpa murmured. "You have changed so much." He held her at arm's length and looked at her. She felt a little embarrassed as he spun her around. He looked up at Sophie's mother, Nascha, and declared, "I can't believe this girl has grown so much since I last saw her."

Grandma Beth smiled in admiration, grabbing Sophie's cheeks in her hands. "You are so pretty, my dear Sophie."

"Oh, Gia Gia, I'm not."

"What!" her grandmother protested. "What did you say?"

Sophie was now quite embarrassed. "Gia Gia, I'm not pretty. But I know you love me."

Her grandmother looked astonished at this statement, but let it go for the moment, saying, "Well, you have one thing right. I do love you. That's for sure." She hugged Sophie even tighter, and Sophie hugged her back, hard.

The Surprise

Sophie's mother, Nascha, watched all of this love and excitement with a huge grin on her face. After things calmed down, Sophie sat down between her grandparents. They were so glad to see her that her grandmother patted her hand and her grandfather smoothed her hair.

"E-mailing each other is good, but this is what I truly wanted. I wanted to see my girl in person," said her grandfather. "There is nothing like the real thing, huh kiddo?" He called her kiddo a lot and she loved it.

Sophie's grandparents were archaeologists. Sophie had found that when she told her friends her grandparents were archeologists, no one quite believed her because none of their grandparents did anything quite so interesting.

They had been teaching at a university in England and were studying a "dig" of an old castle. They often e-mailed her pictures of what they were doing and finding.

Her grandparents explained that since the project was over, they had come back to the States. They had hurriedly dropped their suitcases at their house across town and had come right over to see her.

"Wow!" Sophie exclaimed, throwing her hands up in the air, "This is just about the best surprise I've ever had." Everyone laughed, and Mom went to fetch the cookies from the kitchen for all.

Chapter 3
Surprise Number Two

As everyone ate cookies and drank iced tea, Sophie's grandfather spoke. "Well, my girl," he said, patting her knee, "being here is only part of the surprise."

"What do you mean?" Sophie asked, looking up into his face.

"Well, your mom, dad, and grandmother and I have been talking."

"Yes," her mom added, "and your grandparents have something to ask you."

"What's that?" Sophie asked.

"Honey, we had just finished this excavation we were doing in England when a good friend of ours called us from Greece. It seems he has made what he believes is a monumental discovery there."

Sophie's grandmother took over. "Yes, our friend Professor Conrad is in Greece and he thinks he has found a temple buried on a place that no one has explored before."

Sophie was listening to this, but did not like the sound of where the conversation was heading. Was she going to get her grandparents back, only to have them turn around and leave again?

As her grandmother continued talking she pulled the laptop computer that was on the table closer so they all could see. She opened the computer and her fingers ran across the keyboard with practiced skill.

Grandma Beth then showed them a picture of what looked like an ordinary hill. Sophie looked at the picture, carefully. She saw a large hill with a tree nearby where sheep were peacefully grazing on the grass. "Yes," Sophie acknowledged, "it looks just like an ordinary old hill."

Her grandmother pushed a key and a different picture appeared. It showed a man standing next to that same hill where two tall Greek columns of stone had now been unearthed. There were stones everywhere on the ground, and the hill looked like someone had taken a big bite out of it.

"Well, that's wonderful," Sophie muttered. Then she blurted out, "You're not going to leave me again, are you?" She knew her voice carried that whine of displeasure that sometimes surfaces when you're holding back a lot of emotion.

"No, we're not," her grandfather, said. "We are not going to Greece unless …" and here he paused a bit "…unless you come with us."

Sophie stared blankly at her grandfather. She looked to her mother with a look on her face that seemed to say, "What did he just say?" Sophie was not quite sure she understood.

"Sophie," her mother explained, "your grandparents are trying to tell you that they want to take you to Greece with them. They would make it a working vacation. They could help their friend and have time to vacation with you and explore Greece. You would all be together."

What they were saying was finally making sense to Sophie. But, quite honestly, she was experiencing some mixed feelings about what they had just asked her to do. What about those amazing big summer plans she had been looking forward to having? No sleepovers. No amusement park rides. No hanging out with her best friends. Everything certainly would change.

On the other hand, she had been hearing about Greece her

whole life. Beth and Dimitri's families were originally from Greece and had learned to speak Greek growing up. As long as she could remember, her dad, Mihalis, loved to tell stories about Greek history. Now she would be able to actually go there and see it for herself. That would be pretty awesome.

Sophie was unaware that she had grown quiet while pondering her dilemma. She saw that everyone was staring at her, obviously wondering what she was thinking.

As if she had been reading Sophie's mind, her mother said, "You need to be realistic about this, honey. Greece is too far away to change your mind if you should get there and decide you want to come home."

She continued, "Things are different in Greece where you will be staying. You will be able to use the computer and e-mail dad, all your friends, and me. However, you need to know that you will not be able to text message your friends or use the cell phone as much as you do now. It would be too expensive."

Sophie sat quietly on the couch, still thinking. "Just what," she thought to herself, "do I want to do?"

Then it happened again. That same warm feeling in her chest started. And this time she also felt a kind of tingling sensation in her body. "What was this feeling about?" she wondered. The last time she felt it, which had been just a short time ago, it had been related to the feeling of being connected to all her friends. So, what did it mean?

Sophie kept thinking, the thoughts rolling through her mind. "This is an adventure, and you don't know what will happen." Suddenly a new thought popped into her head. "So, what are you waiting for? Say, YES, and just GO! It's what you want to do. Go, Sophie. Go!"

Everyone watched her face, waiting to see what she was going to decide. Her mother started to speak, and Sophie knew what she was going to tell her—she didn't have to go if she didn't want to.

Sophie loudly and passionately announced, "I'm going." Then she smiled and laughed, and said it even louder because everyone was looking at her like they hadn't understood what she had just said. "I AM GOING WITH YOU!"

Now, they all seemed to be talking at once. Sophie could not keep up with what they were saying. Her mother asked one more time, "Are you sure?" That was her way. She was always cautious and serious.

"Yes, Mom. I want to go."

"Okay," she said. "Call your father and tell him. He couldn't get away from work today and he'll want to know what has happened." Everyone was so excited that even her mother was beginning to smile. As Sophie pulled out her purple phone to call her dad she could hear them all talking and making plans.

There were only three days before they had to leave. They must call the professor who had invited them and tell him they were coming. Everything was happening so quickly. It was exciting!

Her grandparents were getting ready to go and told her they would call this evening with more instructions for what Sophie would need to pack for the trip. Did she have her passport? Yes, oh good. They had forgotten to ask that before. They stood and started moving toward the front door.

They fondly patted Sophie's back, as if they could not bear to leave her again, even if it was only for three days. Everyone kissed one another's cheeks and hugged. As her father had explained to her when she was just a little girl, "You are part of a Greek family, so that means lots of kissing and hugging and affection." Boy, was he ever right, especially today.

They all went outside. Her grandparents and her mom were still talking about what she needed to bring, how she should pack it, what other arrangements needed to be made—on and on and on. She still had not even called her dad to tell him the news.

Sophie waved goodbye to her grandparents. They were still grinning and talking excitedly as they drove down the driveway. She knew in her heart that she was doing the right thing. She smiled to herself. She was going to Greece, dig up an old temple, and have her grandparents all to herself. She was one lucky girl.

Chapter 4

Getting Ready to Go to Greece

The next three days flew by. Sophie's dad taught World History at the local university and he had taken time off work to be with Sophie and her mom. They made a list of what she would need and set out to do some shopping.

Sophie needed new shoes and more shorts for warm sunny days. Plus a couple of sweaters and long sleeve shirts for cool evenings. They discovered her backpack had a hole in it, which meant she needed a new one.

They went to the bookstore and bought a number of books for her to take with her—just in case the television that was in the rented house where they were going to be living did not work. This was her parents' backup plan in case she needed something to do. She chose a book on Greek mythology and a number of other books, including one about the mysteries and temples of Greece.

Every day was busy. Besides, all of her girlfriends wanted to see her before she left. One by one they made their appearance at the house, sometimes coming to visit in two's and three's.

There was no doubt they would miss her a lot. She had to promise each one of them she would send e-mails to keep them up to date on what she was doing. They had to promise to write back, too.

The day came when Sophie had to organize all the things she needed to take with her, so she spread everything out on her bed. It was covered with clothes, underwear, socks, books, and lots of other things her mother had put together.

Sophie's dad came in and said that he was going to help with the packing. She was glad that she didn't have to figure it out by herself. He sat down on the edge of the bed and announced that he had a little gift for her.

With that, he handed her a package. She tore off the plain white tissue paper, which meant he had wrapped the gift himself. Inside was a pad of drawing paper and a large set of more than a hundred colored pencils.

"Oh, Dad!" she exclaimed. "This is just what I need. The set I have is old and the pencils are short. This will work to draw pictures of what I see and then I can send them back on the computer."

He smiled, but for the first time she saw that he was a little sad. "Dad, what's wrong?"

"Well, Sophie, I think it's wonderful that you're going to have this experience. But," he paused, "I'm going to miss you a lot."

Sophie was rather surprised. As serious as her mother was, her father was just the opposite. He was funny and light-spirited. He laughed a lot and enjoyed life. He was good for her mom because she needed to laugh more, and her dad saw to it that she did.

Her dad always told Sophie stupid knock-knock jokes, even though she thought she was too old to be playing that game. He had always made time to be with her each day when she was little.

Now, she was the one that was too busy. Still, he would always say, "Well, sweetie pie, how about next week we have a Dad-and-Sophie-only day?" She would miss that this summer.

Her father had grey eyes and dark hair that curled when it was hot outside, just the way hers did. He was not tall, but he carried himself in such a way that people always seemed to respect him.

Sophie thought her dad must be one of the smartest fathers in the world. He knew so much because he taught and studied world history. Instead of making it boring and dull with the memorization of dates and such, he told wonderful stories. He used to tell her those stories before she went to bed when she was a little girl.

Her dad always said that the best villains as well as heroes were in history. There were stories of bravery and courage. The greatest love stories ever told, both happy and sad, were in history. It was all there if you knew where to look.

Seeing her father look so sad sitting there on her bed all covered with the clothes she was going to take with her, she began to feel sad, too. Sophie felt tears well up in her eyes, and she went to him and hugged him.

He looked into her face. "Sophie, you know that I love you. You will always be my special girl." She clung to him now, a large tear sliding down her face.

In the long mirror on her closet door she could see the reflection of the two of them sitting next to each other on the bed. Looking at her image in the mirror, he said, "You are becoming a young woman, Sophie. Just look how pretty you are."

But Sophie looked away from her image in the mirror. "Oh, Dad, I don't feel pretty."

"What on earth do you mean?" he asked, as if he couldn't believe what she was saying.

Sophie sat up a little straighter and looked hard at herself in the mirror. "Dad, just look at me."

He looked in the mirror, staring at her reflection. "What do you see, Sophie, that you don't like?"

"Oh, Dad!" she groaned. "I just don't look like some of the other girls. I'm smaller than my friends. My hair gets all frizzy when I'm hot, and my nose is too big. I don't like the color of my skin and I don't like the way my face is shaped."

Her father tilted his head as he thoughtfully gazed at her image in the mirror. Sophie could see by the way he looked at her that he could not quite grasp what she was talking about, but that he was trying hard to understand.

"Sophie," he said, "I had no idea you felt this way about yourself." Then, because she was feeling the sadness of suddenly leaving and because she was feeling upset about how she looked—another big tear rolled down her cheek.

Her dad turned his head to look at her directly. "Sophie, you need to know that your hair reminds me of your mom's hair, and you know I love her hair."

Inside, Sophie was thinking, "My hair is not like Mom's. It's like yours. Your hair is okay for you, but not for me." But she remained quiet. She didn't voice her thoughts out loud because she knew he wouldn't agree with her.

"And your face. Oh, my goodness. Botticelli would have loved to paint that face." With this, he took the edge of his folded hand, tipped her face upward and with the thumb of his other hand he wiped away another big tear that was creeping down her face.

"Botti who?" she inquired.

"Oh, he was a famous painter."

Again Sophie was unconvinced and silently thought to herself, "I seriously doubt that a famous painter would have liked my face. Why should he? I don't."

"As for your size," her father continued, "I think we just don't know how tall you'll eventually be. You have more time to see how things turn out in that department. You are healthy, Sophie, and too young to know how wonderful that is."

This time Sophie thought he did have a good point. Aloud, she admitted, "You might be right about that."

Then he said, "As for your nose, well, honey, it's a fine nose. It is just like your grandmother's nose. Don't you like your grandmother's nose?

Sophie wrinkled her own nose and admitted, "I like it better on her."

With that, her dad laughed—a hearty big laugh. And somehow it felt good to finally talk about all of this, so Sophie laughed, too.

About this time, her mom poked her head around the corner, knocking faintly at the door. "May I come in?" she asked.

They both answered, "Yes," at the same time, which made them laugh again.

Sophie could see that her mother was holding something in her hand. In Sophie's eyes, her mom was beautiful with her coal black hair tied up in a ponytail.

She pulled up the chair that was next to Sophie's desk and handed Sophie a package wrapped in soft blue tissue paper. Sophie wasted no time in pulling off the paper. She held the contents in her hands and took a long look at it. It was a photograph in a purple frame. It was a picture of her mom and dad with Sophie in the middle. Everyone was smiling and having a good time at the park.

Sophie flew off the bed and gave her mom a big kiss on the cheek. "Thanks, Mom. This is way cool! The purple frame is so ME."

She posed, putting her left hand on her hip and her right hand in the air like a super model, which made everyone laugh one more time.

Sophie held the framed picture out in front of her and took another long look. "I love it so much. I'm not going to put this in the suitcase. It's going to travel with me in my backpack. That way you can both be with me all the time."

With that, they set about packing her bags. The packing project actually was fun, and it came together quickly. In less than an hour, her suitcases were packed and sitting upright near the door, ready to travel. Her parents had given her hugs and left the room. She was now alone.

Her new backpack sat waiting for the finishing touches. She slipped the photo inside, placing it carefully in the middle of the bag. "Now," she thought, "I'm ready to go."

Chapter 5
A Look at Athens

The alarm clock beeped. Sophie's feet hit the floor running. It seemed that she never did completely stop moving that entire morning. She hurriedly dressed while her dad loaded the suitcases into the car.

Mom was doing a last-minute check of the packing list. She stood with her pen in hand, talking aloud to herself as she went down the list. "Passport, check. Money, check." And on she went.

Sophie managed to eat her toast and drink her orange juice as she scurried about putting on her purple flip-flops and double checking her backpack. Yep, everything was there, including the photograph.

Her friends had sent her a gigantic e-mail. They had made a little movie that showed them all holding up a sign saying, 'Have fun this summer.' They were all laughing and giggling as usual, and it made Sophie smile to see them acting so silly. Since she barely had time to watch the movie, she forwarded it to her grandmother's computer. This way she could watch it again and again while she was in Greece.

Soon they were all out the door, in the car, and on their way.

Chapter 5

Her dad was driving, probably a little too fast. They traveled across town to the airport, and her dad dropped Sophie and her mother at the door, while he went to park the car.

Sophie's grandparents were already there, and everyone said a quick "Hi" as they headed for the check-in counter. Dimitri proudly announced that he was using his frequent flyer miles to upgrade them to first-class seats. He said he was just too old to fly clear across the ocean in a small seat anymore.

By the time they got the tickets and checked their bags, it was time to bid her parents farewell. Sophie was afraid she might cry once she thought about leaving home and actually saying good-bye to her parents. So, it was a relief when she and her grandparents had to hustle through security and get to their assigned gate. There was simply no time for tears. After quick hugs and kisses, she found herself waving to her parents as she traveled up the escalator backwards so she could see them one last time.

It seemed like no time at all until she was boarding the plane. The seats in first class were huge, and now she understood what her grandfather had meant. This was truly a luxurious way to fly.

Sophie settled into her awesome recliner. She had a big pillow, a nice little blanket, and her own little TV screen for movies and such. The plane took off as though it were floating into the sky—amazing since it was so big.

Her grandfather leaned across the aisle, patted her hand and asked, "How are you doing, kiddo?" She was terrific, she was fine, and she could not believe she was traveling to Greece.

Hours later, when she had looked at everything she wanted to see on her TV, eaten her food, and stretched her legs a couple of times, she was reminded of how, when she was a little girl, she used to ask from the backseat of the car, "Are we there yet?"

Unfortunately, she found out from the flight attendant that there were several more hours of flying time. "Bummer," she thought to herself.

She looked around and noticed that everyone seemed to be dropping off to sleep. Try as she would, she couldn't go to sleep. She squirmed around in her seat and finally took the picture of her parents out of her backpack. She set it on her little table where it was easy to see. That made her feel more peaceful, and somewhere over the Atlantic Ocean her eyes must have closed and she finally fell asleep.

How long she had slept she didn't know, but her grandmother was now trying to wake her up. Wow, had she actually managed to fall asleep?

Before Sophie knew it, the plane landed and she was, according to the flight attendant's announcement, in Athens, Greece. It was official. Once the cabin bell sounded, everyone was on their feet. The passengers around her were pulling out bags and her grandmother squeezed over and said, "Honey, you need to stay close to me. This is a busy airport, and it can be overwhelming. So keep a close eye on me."

"You bet," Sophie promised, as she grabbed her stuff.

In an instant, they were off the plane, and it seemed to Sophie that they were running and stopping, running and stopping. Then, a big official-looking man in a dark blue uniform was stamping her passport, and she was on her way with her grandparents to claim their luggage.

Soon it seemed there were people everywhere. There were relatives hugging one another with joy and happiness and babies bouncing in parents' arms, some crying, and people running from place to place.

Sophie knew they were looking for a man named Nikos, a friend of her grandparents. She saw Nikos before they did. He was holding up a sign with her grandfather's name, Dimitri Mangos, on it.

Nikos had black hair, sparkling dark eyes, and a big black mustache sitting over a smiling mouth full of big white teeth. He wore jeans and a short-sleeved white shirt. He looked fresh and ready for a busy day.

They all started moving toward Nikos, and when he saw them he broke into a run to reach them, grabbing her grandfather first. They held onto each other like two old bears patting each other on the back and speaking in Greek.

It was Gia Gia's turn, and Nikos respectfully kissed her on both cheeks while they laughed at something funny he must have said. He then turned to Sophie. "So, this is the beautiful Sophie I have heard so much about." He made the word *beautiful* stretch and hang in the air when he said it. She was embarrassed and felt the heat come into her cheeks, turning her face bright red. She knew she wasn't beautiful.

Nikos ignored her red face and instead shouted, "Yasoo!" He

raised his arms into the air greeting them, "Yasoo! And welcome to my country!" Sophie had to laugh, because as she looked around at the crowds of people, it seemed that absolutely everyone was talking with their hands.

Sophie's grandmother had laughingly warned her about Nikos. She pointed out that he was quite a character and very dramatic. And that he never seemed to meet a person he did not like.

Her grandparents had known Nikos for many years. Whenever they were at a loss as to how or where to find a certain tool or piece of equipment for the archaeological site, Nikos could always find a way to get what was needed, even when everyone said it was impossible. Her grandmother added that he truly had a pure heart.

They began walking with Nikos to where the van was parked. "Okay," Nikos cheered excitedly rubbing his hands together. "Are we going to the Parthenon today for Sophie?"

Her grandfather had warned them that they would 'hit the ground running' when they got to Athens. Yes, the flight had been a long one, but since they had all slept on the way, no one felt tired.

Sophie learned that the plan had changed because there had been new developments at the archeological site. Professor Conrad, the man whom they were going to assist with his excavation, had told them that in his wildest dreams he had never seen a more beautiful temple than the one he had recently discovered. A new statue had also been discovered as well as some other things that he wouldn't talk about on the phone. "You just have to see it to believe it," he explained.

So, the new plan was that today they would travel up to the ruins called the Parthenon so Sophie could see it. After that they would stop for food, and then Nikos would drive them straight to the site, arriving late tonight. This was something they had originally planned to do later, rather than sooner.

Everyone answered Nikos's question about going to the Parthenon all at once. It was a unanimous, "Yes. Let's go!" Nikos hoisted the luggage into the van with virtually no effort at all. He was terribly strong. They all slid into the van, with Sophie sitting up front next to Nikos.

The minute they eased out onto the street in front of the parking garage, things got crazy. Sophie had never seen traffic like this in her life. People were driving like they had lost their minds.

This was Athens, one of the oldest cities in the world and the capital of Greece. Today the traffic was absolutely incredible. The buses, trucks, cars, and vans all seemed to be fighting for space on the same road.

Nikos said that there were over six million people living in Athens and the surrounding areas of the city. It seemed to Sophie that they were all here right now, either honking their horns or wildly waving their arms outside their car windows accompanied by gestures and shouts, or both. To make matters worse, the motorcycles and motor scooters darted in and out of the other vehicles at breakneck speed.

Nikos appeared not to be fazed by this chaos. Sophie was reminded of a film about a bullfighter she had seen on television. The bull would charge; then the matador would turn at the last minute and avoid being killed by swinging his scarlet cape to show he was in control of the bull's dangerous movements. So, too, Nikos skillfully turned the van time and time again, just when Sophie was sure somebody was going to hit them. All that Nikos was missing was a red cape.

Nikos pointed things out to Sophie as they traveled. This was the best bakery in Athens. That was the way to the main market. Most all the signs were in Greek, but a few were in English. The air smelled of exhaust fumes and Nikos kept his driver's side window open in case he had to yell at someone. He honked his horn all the time, but it became a kind of language to Sophie—as if drivers were constantly talking to one another, but not in polite ways. The traffic never stopped, but Nikos took side streets this way and that, traveling toward their destination, claiming he knew a shortcut here and there.

Sophie had read about the Greek people and knew that in ancient times they had built a magnificent temple on top of the Acropolis called the Parthenon. It had to be one of the most famous sites in the world. Now she was going to see the real thing, and she was anxious to get there.

They turned a corner, and Nikos pointed toward an area on top of the hill on their right. There it was. You could see the Parthenon clearly. It overlooked the city and looked down at everyone and everything from its majestic height.

Chapter 5

The temple shone like a brilliant white jewel against the deep azure sky. It appeared to be square, and you could see the many columns that made up its walls.

Then, they had to drive in front of buildings that blocked the view. It was like playing a game, constantly looking, and waiting for the Parthenon to peek out from behind apartment buildings and hotels and office buildings as they wound their way upward, getting closer and closer. It would not be long now until they reached the temple.

Chapter 6
Athens and the Parthenon

Sophie bounced out of the front seat, glad they had at last made it through all the traffic. They moved forward, joining the many people climbing the stairs that led to the Parthenon's entrance.

Nikos now seemed to feel that because this was his country, he should be her personal guide. He made them all stop. "Now, before you get any closer, drink in this gorgeous sight."

He was right to make them stop and absorb the view. Other tourists were listening to their guides preparing them for their tours. It would have been easy to be distracted by the surrounding activity.

They all stopped to look up at the building stretching gracefully toward the sky. "Never forget this moment," Nikos advised Sophie. "You are going to travel back into history." Sophie thought of her father and how he would have loved being here with them today.

Nikos raised his hands as if he were conducting an invisible symphony. "Sophie, you are standing on sacred ground—ground that's special." His mustache seemed to wiggle as he spoke. Sophie didn't laugh; instead she absorbed the deep feelings conveyed in his words.

Chapter 6

Slowly, in spite of the many people around them, they walked up the stairs. With each step, the columns seemed to grow larger. The brilliant sunlight made the columns look white. The air seemed cleaner. A fresh breeze lifted her hair off her shoulders. This place certainly did feel different than any place she had ever been before.

"Nikos, how old is this place?" Sophie asked.

"It is extremely old—thousands of years old, Sophie." Nikos spoke the words quietly, as if to not disturb the past.

"Think," Nikos said, walking into the top area. He stopped to look around. "Think of how many people have stood where you are today, Sophie." She thought about the thousands of years and millions of people, and it was hard to wrap her mind around those numbers.

"Why did people come here?" she asked Nikos.

He took a deep breath, as if he were just getting started. "Because this is not just any old temple, my dear—this was the home of a goddess. She resided inside these columns, inside these walls."

"These columns are white now, but it might surprise you to know that this was once a colorful building." He pointed up to the fragments of carvings on panels that were just beneath the roof. "Those panels were covered with statues playing out scenes from mythology."

"Taken," Nikos explained, "by Englishmen. The missing things are now in the city of London." Sophie thought it was rather sad that so much was missing since it all belonged to this building and to Greece.

Nikos continued, "Long ago these columns were painted red and yellow, and all the major primary colors. In fact, all the white marble statues you see were once brightly painted. The Greeks loved colorful buildings and statues."

They all turned and slowly moved into the interior of the space, then crossed over the threshold. The columns were all around them. Sophie realized that standing on this floor held a feeling she never could have guessed existed by just looking at pictures. It was a feeling of the Ancients themselves.

Nikos pointed behind them. "Imagine that there were huge doors stretching upward back there." Then he turned to look at the back of the temple. "There were once walls that enclosed the magnificent statue. It was no ordinary statue." He raised his hand and clenched his fist. "Look! The statue," he said, "was of the great Goddess Athena."

"Athena!" he repeated quite loudly. Sophie looked around to see if anyone else was listening. No one was. "She stood thirty-eight feet high, and her skin, some say, looked like ivory. Gold covered her body, and she wore a large helmet of gold, too. Do you know how much gold was put on that statue?"

"No," Sophie answered. "How much?"

Nikos replied with immense energy in his voice, "Two thousand five hundred pounds of gold." Sophie had to admit that was a lot of gold.

"Imagine that it is dark inside except for the light cast by burning torches. The air would be filled with the aroma of sweet incense. Athena had been placed at the back of the temple, filling up the space from floor to ceiling. She stood with her right hand turned upward, her arm outstretched. Balanced on her hand was an image that today would look to us like an angel."

"The angel, in fact, was Nike, another goddess—the Goddess of Victory. She represented victory over fears, victory over limitations. She, too, was covered in gold—her dress swirled and her feathered wings spread."

"She looked like she had just lightly landed in Athena's outstretched hand," Nikos whispered into Sophie's ear. "The shield at her side was gigantic, and an enormous python snake lay at her ankle. Can you imagine her?" he asked. "Can you see her, Sophie?"

Sophie gazed at the empty space where Athena once stood. Softly, she asked Nikos, "Where is the statue now?"

Nikos shook his head as if he felt sad to have to tell her. "Gone. Some say that she was taken to another country where she was destroyed. But no one really knows what happened to her."

By now Sophie was so deeply engrossed in the experience of Nikos' story that she had quite literally forgotten about her grandparents.

She saw that her grandfather was in the process of trying to direct them all out of the building. Sophie turned to look again at the empty space where the statue had stood so many centuries before. She turned to Nikos, "This was her house then, this building?"

Chapter 6

"Yes, and more," he said. "The statue itself was where she stayed when she was here on earth."

"She lived in the statue?" Sophie asked. Her eyes got big just thinking about it.

"Yes," Nikos reported. "The Ancients believed this to be true. That is why the statue had to be pure."

Sophie turned to all of the adults. "You go on ahead outside; I'm going to stay in here a little longer." They all seemed to accept her decision and went outside to look at the building from different angles.

Sophie wondered what the statue of Athena had originally looked like. She wished she had a picture. She found an isolated little spot and sat down on the stone floor. The columns stretched up around her, and she found herself just staring at the empty space on the temple floor. She grew quiet inside, as none of the tourists walking about seemed to even see her.

Sophie closed her eyes and tried to imagine the statue of Athena.

Instantly, she felt a funny feeling. Something was happening to her. Her body started to feel warm and tingly. It was as if her heart seemed to open like a flower to the sun. It was the same feeling she remembered having on that first day of summer vacation when she thought about her closeness with her friends. And it was the same feeling she had felt when she knew she absolutely wanted to come on this trip.

Sophie opened her eyes, and to her amazement the scene that Nikos had described was right there before her. She could actually see, with her eyes wide open, in the dim light the commanding statue of Athena.

What magic spell had Nikos cast over her? Was this a dream or was this real? She could clearly see Athena standing there—handsome, confident, and bold. She stood tall and was covered in golden clothing.

Nikos had told her earlier that Athena had been a leader, a teacher, and a friend to the heroes and heroines of old. He said that she could call upon the powers of both war and peace. She loved artists and creativity. She was thought to be the finest weaver of cloth in the celestial world.

Looking at her image was dazzling to Sophie's eye. Then something quite unexpected happened. Athena seemed to turn her head ever so slightly. She looked right at Sophie. It was as if the statue were alive and that she actually knew Sophie was there in her temple.

Across time and space, Athena looked straight into Sophie's eyes. Athena nodded her head slightly with just a hint of a smile on her self-assured lips. She then turned and looked straight ahead across her temple once more.

In the next instant, the space was empty. But the feeling of warmth in Sophie's body lingered.

What had happened? Why had Athena nodded at her? What was Athena trying to say? Was Athena acknowledging her in some mysterious way? Had she seen into the past for a couple of seconds? Or, was it her overly active imagination? Whatever it was, she would never forget it.

Sophie got up from her little corner on the floor. Slowly she walked out of the temple, deeply engrossed in her own thoughts.

She had no trouble finding her grandparents and Nikos. They were chatting while walking over to another lovely building. Nikos called it the Erechtheum. This building had an unusual feature. It had a kind of patio attached to it, and the columns that held up the roof were statues of goddesses carved from marble.

The sculptor had carved the goddesses' clothes as if they were moving in an unseen breeze. For Sophie, though, nothing would ever compare to what she had just experienced.

The sun had climbed higher and the heat more intense. She felt herself getting tired. Her grandmother seemed to notice and asked, "Sophie is anything wrong?"

She wanted to say, "No, nothing is wrong. But let me tell you what just happened. You are not going to believe it!"

Dimitri spoke up before she could say a word. "I think she's hungry, that's all." Food was her grandfather's solution to all problems. She guessed that Nikos had the same solution to problems, because he loudly agreed. "You're right. We need to eat. I know a perfect little taverna not far from here."

He was excited now, as was Sophie's grandfather. The two of them, having found agreement, were walking toward the van. Sophie's grandmother turned to follow, but put her arm around Sophie's shoulders. "Are you sure you're okay, my dear?"

"Yes, but I have something to ask you."

Sophie's grandmother stopped to listen.

"I just want you to promise me something."

Her grandmother looked down into Sophie's face, straight into her eyes and, it seemed, straight into her heart.

"What is it?" her grandmother asked.

"I must return to this place before I leave Greece to go home. I have to come back here. Can we do that, Gia Gia?"

"Of course," her grandmother said, fondly patting her shoulder. "I'll personally bring you back." With that she swept her hand from one side of the plaka to the other, stopping at the Parthenon. "It is a fantastic place, isn't it?"

"Yes!" Sophie said, gazing through the columns of the temple to the place where she had seen the Goddess Athena. "It certainly is!"

Chapter 7
Traveling Back in Time

They stopped for food at the small taverna Nikos had mentioned and ate on the outside patio overlooking the city. The Parthenon was still glowing in the sun. The columns had now turned a golden-honey color.

Nikos and her grandparents continued talking about their past adventures. They seemed to take turns telling stories about each other, and many were hilarious.

Sophie thought they had ordered too much food, but they ate it all. She, though, would not touch the olives. She did not like them and it didn't matter what color they were. No olive would ever touch her lips—which amused the grown-ups.

When they got back in the van to leave the city, Sophie let her grandfather sit up front with Nikos. She climbed into a back seat to be by herself. She took her journal out of her trusty backpack and wrote about her experience at the Parthenon.

Sophie described everything she had seen and felt in her 'daydream,' although it seemed like so much more. She felt a secret thrill just remembering and writing about it. She wrote in large letters: WHAT WAS ATHENA TRYING TO TELL ME? She underlined it three times before she fell asleep.

When Sophie woke up, they had been traveling for several hours. Nikos announced that they were close to the house he had rented for them. It was dark now and the sky looked like it was full of diamonds. The old road was full of bumps and ruts, and they bounced along through the darkness.

Eventually, they turned onto a dusty driveway; even dustier than the road they had been driving on. They drove up to a well-lit house, and a tall, stately woman came out to greet them.

She was wearing a chocolate-brown dress and an apron adorned with little orange flowers. She had her dark hair pulled up and twisted into a bun at the back of her head. Sophie thought she looked stern and unfriendly.

However, when Nikos got out of the van, a big smile spread across her face and she ran to meet him, clasping his outstretched hands as he kissed her on the cheek. Everyone got out of the van, their legs stiff from sitting so long.

Nikos walked over to the woman. "May I introduce you to Nina? This house has been in her family a long time." Nina nodded her head in agreement. "While you are staying here, Nina is going to be your housekeeper," he said, looking over at her grandparents.

This was a new revelation to Sophie. No one had mentioned this to her and she wondered how it would work out. But her grandparents shook Nina's hand and seemed happy with the idea. Then, Nikos calmly presented Sophie to Nina, who shook her hand and simply said in her accented English, "Welcome to the Blue House. May it be your happy home."

Everyone pulled bags out of the van and went into the house. It did not take Sophie long to pick out the room she wanted. Someone had hand-painted a scene of a Greek temple with a picture of a woman on the wall. Sophie would have preferred a picture of a goddess, although, it was a nice painting.

The moon had risen and it shone into the window of her room flooding it with silver light. In spite of how long she had slept in the van, as soon as she touched the soft bed she was asleep again. The next morning Sophie came bounding down the stairs, full of energy. Nina was in the kitchen waiting for her. She promptly cooked her some scrambled eggs and sliced homemade bread she had baked the day before.

Sophie's grandparents had already eaten and were on their computers. Her grandmother came back into the kitchen, carrying her portable laptop computer and played a video for her that her dad had made of himself and her mom waving goodbye, wishing her well.

She had called them after they landed at the Athens airport to let them know they had arrived safely. "Well, young lady, eat up because we are finally going to go see this archaeological wonder that Professor Conrad wants to show us."

That was all it took. Sophie was in her room plowing through her suitcase. In no time she had put on her favorite khaki shorts and tangerine shirt. She tied her hair up in a bright orange scrunchie, grabbed her sunglasses and sun hat, and went flying back down the stairs.

While walking to the site, her grandmother explained that the whole area was filled with ruins, most of which had never been excavated. They climbed over hills and past old twisted olive trees. The soil was dry, but in spite of this, wildflowers were booming all around them, adding bursts of yellow and orange and sometimes purple. It was a beautiful morning and the sky was clear and the air fresh.

After walking quite a distance, they rounded the top of another hill and looked down and saw it. The mound Sophie had seen in the photograph on the computer back in her living room was right there below her. A stocky man leaning on a shovel waved enthusiastically and walked briskly toward them. His body looked muscular and strong, his hair white and long, and he had a broad smile on his face. He wore black glasses balanced on a large prominent nose framing his happy face.

"This must be Professor Conrad," Sophie thought.

He swung his hand forward and clasped hands with her grandfather. "Dimitri! Great to see you at last!" he said excitedly to her grandfather. "How long has it been?"

"Ten years," her grandfather answered. "Ten years too long, if you ask me." The two old friends seemed happy to see one another.

"Beth!" He reached out and clasped her grandmother's hands.

"My heavens, it is good to see you." He hugged her briefly and then took a long, lingering look at her as if he could not believe he was seeing her at last.

Her grandmother motioned for Sophie to come over. "This is my Sophie," she announced fondly.

"How wonderful to meet you," he exclaimed.

He said this as if she, too, were a long lost friend. He directed them all over to the mound. "Come on over now. Let's look at what I've found."

He could barely contain his pleasure. Sophie was walking next to Professor Conrad and as she looked over her shoulder, she saw that her grandparents were holding hands. It was clear to Sophie that they were happy to be back in Greece and happy to be there with each other.

The mound was much larger than it had looked in the picture. It would have been easy to see this as nothing other than an ordinary hill. Yet, as they rounded the corner, they could see how the earth was piling up off to the side. Men were already at work this morning, digging dirt out of the hillside and using wheelbarrows to cart it over to the edge of a narrow road. The surrounding ground was littered with piles of stones and rocks that had been moved out of the way of the excavation.

Then Sophie saw it. It took her breath away. She let out a loud "Ahhhh!" as she looked at the delicate ruins emerging from the ground where the men were working. Sophie saw two slender white columns that glistened against the dark earth. They were tall and graceful, and connected at the top. What actually caught Sophie's attention was a statue standing next to the columns—a statue of a woman, tall and upright.

Sophie recognized her at once. This was no ordinary woman. It was Athena. After her experience in the Parthenon, she would have recognized Athena anywhere.

How wonderful! The goddess was back in her life again. Sophie took a long look at the statue. She was taller than a real woman— almost seven feet. She stood on a short pedestal and was gazing straight ahead. Her helmet was on her head, her shield at her side, and an owl sat on her shoulder. Sophie knew from what she had read that the owl was Athena's special companion, as well as a symbol of her wisdom.

Everyone looked at the exquisite statue standing before them. Her face was strong and revealed caring. Every detail was perfect, from the curls of her hair to her graceful outstretched hands, which seemed to say, "Come closer."

Sophie thought about the question she had written in her journal. "What was Athena trying to tell her?" There must be something she wanted Sophie to know.

The professor told them that there was a kind of mystery about how they had found Athena. He went on to explain. "It is rare to find a statue standing upright, rather than lying on the ground. We usually find them with broken hands and generally with the head missing. Not this time, though. We found her buried under the ground just as you see her now."

The professor further explained that finding Athena like this was obviously no accident. It seemed the Ancients had deliberately preserved her just like she had been found. He explained how they had packed earth around the statue and then poured sand into the opening, forming a kind of insulation. Then, they finished by packing more earth around the core they had created. The professor said that they had also found the columns buried in the same way.

"I do not understand what it means. I have never seen this before," continued Professor Conrad.

Sophie was intently listening when a thought crossed her mind. "This reminds me of a time capsule," she said. "You see, at my school they built a new wing on the building. Our principal thought it would be a terrific idea to create a time capsule to dedicate the new addition to our school. So, he asked us to bring to school different items that were important to us."

"We brought in lots of stuff and we all wrote letters. It was kind of a contest, and only the best things and the best letters were chosen. Afterwards, the science teacher wrapped everything very carefully, pumped all the air out of the box to make a vacuum that would preserve everything for the future, and then sealed the box."

Sophie went on with her story. "The box was put in a hollow cornerstone of the building, and it will be there as part of the building for as long as the building stands. Someday, in the future, when that box is opened, people can see what was important to us kids when we created our time capsule."

"I think, from the way you describe it, that these people pre-served this temple as a time capsule for the future, for us to see. It must have been important to them if they went to all of this effort, don't you think?"

The professor glanced over his shoulder, peering across the top of his glasses at her grandparents. "I think we have a future archaeolo-gist here, don't you?" Sophie's grandparents smiled and even laughed a little. Sophie could tell they liked that idea.

"You might be right, Sophie," Professor Conrad said. "But there's more." He pointed out that next to the statue of Athena was a place that had been cleared of earth. The next layer of dirt was yet to be removed. They carefully examined the spot where he was pointing and saw, peeking out of the earth, a small section of marble. It looked like the edge of a foot.

"Look!" he exclaimed. "I think we may find another statue next to Athena." Sophie wondered what or who it could be? The professor pointed out that they would to have to plan how they were going to remove the earth and wanted her grandparents to help.

He also pointed out that the base of the statue of Athena showed that they needed to dig deeper because it looked to him like the floor was still beneath them, covered by earth. Dimitri got down on his knees and looked more closely and thought that the professor was right.

The professor led them over to a wooden table that had been placed under a long open tent. He moved a tray containing things found lying on top of the earth that had just been removed.

Unique arrangements of clay discs were spread out on the tray. He picked several up and placed one in everyone's hand, including Sophie's.

"Now, take a look," he instructed. Sophie turned it around in her hand and looked at it more closely. The back of the disc was flat, but the front had a raised dimensional image on it. On her disc was a four-petal flower. She looked over at her grandmother's and saw that it had a shell design. Then, she saw an owl on the disc her grandfather held in his hand.

The professor continued. "If the people buried this temple on purpose, as I believe they did, then I think they placed these discs over the top of the mound they made. They were placed about six inches apart, with every other disc having a flower design. All of the other images were placed in between the flowers."

"This means that there was a row of flowers, then a row of owls, flowers again, and then a row of shells or one of the other designs we found." As if this surprised him, he said, "They covered them with more earth and then the whole space must have been made into a large grassy hill."

The professor pulled up some chairs and took out a large bottle of water from a nearby ice chest. When everyone was seated under the cool shade of the tent, he set cold glasses of water down in front of each person.

Sophie asked the professor how he had found this place. He chuckled. "The way all significant archeological sites are found are by accident." The adults all laughed at the joke implied by this statement because in spite of lots of planning, things found by accident always seem to be the best.

Professor Conrad explained, "A shepherd brought his sheep to this area to graze because the grass was so plentiful. He fell asleep under a tree, but was soon startled awake by one of his sheep making an awful fuss. The sheep had wandered to the top of the hill and fell in a hole where ground had caved in and could not get out.

"The shepherd had to work hard to get the critter out of the hole. After he did, he noticed these discs of clay, and he immediately knew they were old. The shepherd went home and called me because, believe it or not, we are cousins. This land belongs to my family. In fact, I have a vineyard not far from here."

"I was coming down to this area to check on my vineyard, and since I oversee my family's land, I decided to take a look at what my cousin had found. That's how it all started. I took one look at that mound and I knew something was buried there. So, I started digging after receiving funding from the University of Athens. I found the columns right away and then found the statue just before you left the United States."

He looked again at the clay disc in his hand and Sophie looked at the owl disc in her grandfather's hand. "Isn't the owl supposed to belong to Athena?" she asked. She pointed over to the Athena statue with the image of an owl sitting on her shoulder.

"Yes, you're correct," the professor replied. "It could mean it's a symbol of Athena."

He acted like he was seeing the owl on her shoulder for the first time. He got up, carrying his glass in one hand and the disc in the other, walked over to the statue, and looked at the large stone owl on Athena's shoulder. Then, he looked down at the disc and seemed to be genuinely amazed. The shape of the owl was exactly the same. The head was the same. Even the feathers and the eyes were the same in design and detail. "It looks like the same artist designed both the statue and the discs."

He let out a sigh that announced that this realization surprised him. "I should have seen this before," he said, looking at Sophie. "But it took your young eyes to catch the details."

"I think I understand something else, too," Sophie declared, unable to hide the excitement in her voice.

The professor peered over the rim of his glasses. "Please, Sophie, don't hold back your ideas. Tell me what you're thinking." Sophie took her journal and a black pencil from her backpack. She drew a series of tiny circles, all in rows. She put an X over every other one. "These are the flower discs." She worked fast, and then held up her sketch." Does this look like the way you found them?"

The professor observed her sketch closely. "Yes, I believe so."

"This reminds me of how you plant a garden—with the seeds all in a row," Sophie said. "I think the decorated discs are seeds and the other ones are just what they show—flowers. I think it's a garden." The three adults stared blankly at her and she began to feel embarrassed.

Yes, they admitted, almost simultaneously, that it was an idea worth thinking about. No one wanted to commit to the thought that her idea might be correct and no one wanted to say it was foolish, either. Finally, the professor said, "You have a good eye, Sophie, and I wouldn't be surprised if you're not on to something."

"If you are correct, I'll give you proper credit in the paper when I write about all of this," he promised, waving his hand to indicate the entire area. As he warmed to the idea, he added, with much more enthusiasm, "Excellent, Sophie, very good!"

Then, he asked a question that he did not expect anyone to answer, "What's growing in this garden, I wonder?"

Chapter 8
The Meeting of Two Friends

Sophie was restless today. She woke up that way, and knew exactly why she was feeling out of sorts. It had started the night before when she read her e-mail from Mackenzie. Her girlfriends were all going to the amusement park today.

When Sophie read those words, she felt that feeling of being left out. Soon, she would be seeing e-mailed photos of her friends having fun at the amusement park. The photos would be coming in on her grandmother's computer, and the thought of it distressed her.

Everyone would be laughing and having such a good time while she was far, far away from it all. Sitting here in her sun-filled bedroom, she felt terribly alone. No doubt this was homesickness. She had started to feel it earlier that week.

Sophie had only been in Greece two weeks. In some ways it felt like no time at all, and in other ways it felt like forever. So, at this moment, if there had been any way to magically get home, she would have gone. This wasn't because she didn't like what she was doing. There were lots of things about being here that she liked.

She had quickly formed a comfortable routine for herself. She would get up in the morning, and she and Nina would decide on breakfast. Then, she would check her e-mails, answer any questions, and send a quick hello to her parents and friends. By the time she finished, Nina would be calling her downstairs to eat.

After breakfast, she would get dressed and walk to the site. Her grandparents had been leaving for the site early every morning. By the second day at the site, she knew everyone's name and a fair bit about their life, just like she knew all her neighbors' names at home.

When Sophie reached the site each day, Nikos would be arriving with the graduate students who were working for the professor. Each morning, Nikos picked up the students who stayed in the village and then took them home late afternoon. The regular workers did the hard physical labor—digging out dirt and hauling rocks. Nikos seemed to oversee their work, as well as do a hundred other things.

Sophie had set out to draw a likeness of the statue of Athena. She was half hoping she would have another daydream, but it had not yet happened. One of the graduate students, Diane, was responsible for drawing every single thing they found in the dig, labeling it, and putting a number on it. Then she placed each piece in a plastic bag and stored it.

Diane, who had seen Sophie sketching, offered to show her some tricks during her lunch break on how to improve her drawing. Sophie was amazed at how much better she did after Diane had worked with her. Diane said that she had a sister Sophie's age and that she missed her.

Sophie had noticed that another graduate student, Wyatt, had shown considerable interest in Diane, but she didn't seem to care about him at all. Wyatt had worked the previous summer digging in Guatemala at a Mayan site, and he had lots of captivating stories. He always told them in ways that were hilariously funny.

Whenever Diane was giving Sophie a lesson, Wyatt was never far away. He acted like he was telling his stories to Sophie, but he was checking out Diane's reactions the whole time.

Nina had found a watercolor set that had been left in the Blue House and had given it to Sophie. One day Diane offered to go with her to the house after work to give her a painting lesson. They spent an amazing afternoon together painting and talking. It had been an awesome day.

The next day Diane could not come home with Sophie, even though she had planned to. The professor wanted her to begin doing some research on the computer in the village. That had ended the painting lessons.

In short, Sophie had painted and drawn and done everything she could think of to keep busy. The second statue still had not been unearthed. Her grandfather had informed her that they were planning to set up a new system before they started to dig again.

Sophie's problem was that she was feeling anxious, bored, and homesick, even though two other graduate students, Stefan and Zander, had shared their handheld video game with her. Nothing seemed to help.

The next day, Sophie came down the stairs, her feet thudding all the way till she got to the kitchen. There she discovered that Nina was baking bread. It smelled wonderful, but Sophie was only half interested.

Because this valley was rich in archaeological ruins, lots of scholars and students and archaeologists had rented the Blue House over the years. Nina rented the house to a variety of guests, and for an extra fee she would act as their housekeeper.

As far as Sophie was concerned, Nina had turned out to be a wonderful addition to the household. She baked bread once a week in an unusual brick oven. She washed the clothes in a modern washer, but refused to use a dryer. She chose, instead, to hang the clothes outside on a line. She thought everything smelled better if it dried in the sun. And she was right. It did.

The guests who stayed in the house were French and Italian and English, plus there were people from the United States and Greece, too. Nina managed to speak all these languages and could cook dishes from every country. She was a fantastic cook. She also waged war daily with the dust that came in, thanks to the dry, dusty driveway and nearby road. Keeping the house dusted and neat was a constant battle.

Nina's husband, George took care of the general upkeep and repairs. He always arrived in a battered old car that looked like it would be a miracle if it made it up the driveway. He called the car

Chapter 8

Pegasus in honor of the fast flying horse of old Greek stories. He knew it was a big joke, considering that the rickety thing could barely move.

Sophie found Nina in the kitchen singing an old Greek song she had learned as a child. It was about a mermaid who fell in love with a sailor, and it had many verses. Even though Sophie did not understand Greek, the ballad always sounded sweet and a little sad to her.

Sophie came into the kitchen and sat down at the table. She put her chin in her hands, looking terribly glum. "Sophie," Nina said cheerfully, "I have a surprise for you today." Sophie barely smiled and waited to find out what it was that Nina might consider a surprise.

"I have a cousin, Métis, in the village where I live. She is a world famous weaver of tapestries. She and her daughter are excellent artists with thread. Their weavings have incredible pictures woven into the material," Nina said with tremendous excitement and then continued.

"Their tapestries are so fine you would think they were alive when you looked at them. They depict stories of Greek gods and goddesses. It is fine-looking work."

Nina was waving her hands around, as she always does when she tells a story. "Well, her daughter's name is Athena, but they call her Tena. Her father named her after the goddess. You see, Goddess Athena's mother's name was Métis also."

"I know how you like to draw, Sophie. I have seen your drawings. I think you'll appreciate the fine work they create. Tena is your age and a nice girl. I have asked her to come here today to take you to her house and show you the remarkable tapestries they make. Besides, it will do you good to be with someone your own age."

It was a surprise Sophie had not seen coming. She was beginning to warm up to the idea. In fact, she felt herself becoming more enthused by the minute. The thought of being with someone her own age felt terrific. It was something she totally missed. She got up from the kitchen table and asked, "When is Tena coming?"

"Well, today, of course," Nina said. "She will be here in maybe an hour or so."

"What about my grandparents? Do they think it's okay for me to go?"

"Oh, yes." Nina waved her arm as if to say nobody cared. "They would like you home for dinner around six o'clock. Do you want to go?"

Sophie was already in the kitchen doorway, ready to head upstairs to change. "Yes, of course I want to go. I'll be downstairs in a flash. I want to change my clothes."

Nina, who was still kneading the bread, smiled. "So far, so good," she thought.

Sophie ran up the stairs to her room, shut the door, and took a quick look in the mirror. She combed her hair and changed her clothes twice, finally settling on a pair of green pants and a bright blue shirt. She chose not to wear her flip-flops because they would undoubtedly be covered with dust from the road. She did not want to ruin them. So, her black pair of sandals would have to do.

All the while she was getting dressed, Sophie kept thinking about the fact that this new friend she was going to meet was named Tena. Was that interesting or what?

Since the Parthenon visit, Athena had continued to pop up. There was that first experience with her at the temple. Then there was the statue being excavated at the new archaeological site. And now, the girl she was going to meet was named Athena. Did all of this mean anything special?

Well, no matter. Sophie did not have time to think about it right now.

As she peered out the window, she saw that Nina was outside hanging up laundry. No one else was in sight, so she ran back upstairs to e-mail her mom about what she was going to do today. She found her trusty camera and threw it into her backpack, too.

Nina had now opened the screen door and was shouting, "Sophie, come downstairs, please."

Sophie flew down the stairs, her feet barely touching the floor. There in the doorway stood a tall handsome girl her own age. She had long black hair, grey eyes, and was wearing a white blouse and a blue skirt with flowers on it. She looked a little shy.

As Sophie stepped up and introduced herself, the girl spoke to her in English and announced that her name was Tena. Relieved, Sophie said with surprise, "Oh, you speak English."

Tena laughed. "Yes, my father taught me. I need to speak it for my family's business."

Chapter 8

Nina took over. "Well, you girls should be on your way if you're going to get back by six tonight. You have a lot to see and talk about."

The girls walked out into the bright morning sunshine and started down the road. They had not gone far before they were getting hot and their feet were covered with dust and grime.

"Sophie, I know another way to get to my house," Tena said. She pointed to a hill behind the Blue House. "Going that direction leads right into the forest and it is so much nicer to walk in there—the trees make it cool and comfortable. Let's take the path through the forest."

Sophie hesitated. Her grandfather had cautioned her about going into the forest. The forest was large in this area, covering many miles. He had warned that it was easy to get lost and had asked her not to go very far into the woods.

Sophie asked, somewhat cautiously, "Tena is it true that you can get lost in the woods?"

"Yes, if you do not know where you're going or which of the many paths to take, you can get lost. I assure you, I know the forest well. I will not let anything happen to you."

Once Tena said that, Sophie felt she could trust her. They immediately headed toward the cool, green forest.

As soon as they walked into the shade of trees, it was pleasantly cool. They followed a well-worn path as they began to walk and talk. Tena explained that when she was a young girl, she had a friend who taught her the ways of the forest. She knew the names of all the flowers and trees and birds.

They had gone only a short distance when Tena announced, "Come with me. There is a stream down this way where we can wash the dust and dirt off our legs."

So, the girls went in the direction of the stream. Sophie heard the soft rushing noise of the water before she actually saw the stream. To get there, they clambered up over large white rocks and then walked down toward the inviting stream that lay before them. It had the magical feeling you read about in fairytales.

The water was clear, with just a hint of light green. As Sophie stood on the stony bank of the shallow stream, she could easily see the bottom. She pulled off her sandals, rolled up her pant legs, and waited for Tena to go first.

Tena let out a little cry of delight as she waded out into the stream. The water climbed to her knees, and she lifted the bottom edge of her skirt and tucked it into her waistband. It was probably still going to get wet, but who cared?

Tena said, "The water feels cold at first, but once you get used to it, it feels good."

They splashed around, rubbing the dust off their legs. The water was moving swiftly, and it did feel good. Tena suddenly exclaimed, "Hey, I'm going to take you to meet a friend of mine. Do you like adventures, Sophie?" She asked it like it was a challenge.

Sophie thought to herself, "Sure. I'm ready." She nodded her head and simply answered, "Yes."

Tena explained that they would walk down the stream to the location where her friend always hung out. She told Sophie to put both pairs of their shoes in her backpack, and they set out wading down the stream in knee deep water.

Sophie looked up at the trees as they walked. They were lush and green and were bent slightly forward, as if bowing to the stream and the force of its life-giving water. The light came filtering through the leaves, making some of them transparent and golden.

When the two reached a certain area, Tena turned to Sophie and touched her finger to her lips, signaling Sophie to keep quiet. "Shhhh," she whispered softly, "we must be quiet now."

The stream began to bend and turn and the edges of the water widened, forming a large pool. It was much deeper here in the middle, so they carefully waded closer to the edge where it only came up to their knees.

Suddenly, Sophie nearly let out one of those "Yikes!" exclamations, but she managed to put her hand over her mouth. There in the pool of water was a reflection of a beautiful sight. From one bank of the river, a tree had grown out across the water. From the opposite shore, another tree had also grown from that bank across the water.

The two trees had come together many years earlier and had become entwined, growing as one tree from their middle section up to the top.

Tena walked closer to Sophie so she could whisper and still be heard. "They are beautiful, aren't they? I made up a story about these two trees."

Chapter 8

"What is it?" Sophie whispered. "Tell me."

"Long ago these two trees fell in love with each other and could not bear to be apart. So each tree, year after year, bent a little further over the water, until one day they met in the middle and were finally together. They grew together, as one tree, so they would never be apart."

Sophie was a romantic by nature and adored a good love story like most girls her age. Tena's story, coupled with the beauty of the trees, touched her heart.

"My friend," Tena said, "is on the other side of this tree. If we walk quietly, you can meet him."

The whole time they had been walking through the cool water, Sophie had assumed Tena was taking her to meet a person. The amused tone in Tena's voice now made her think it might be something else.

She followed Tena as quietly as she could, trying not to make noise as the water slapped around her legs. When they reached the Sweetheart Trees, they leaned against the trunk. Tena peered over the tree section and pointed to something sitting on an old, black tree stump in the middle of the water. Sophie balanced herself by leaning on the tree for support and looked in the direction of Tena's hand.

What she saw, perfectly poised on the black mossy tree stump, was a large chelona. The big shell on the turtle's back was black and grey and brown. Its legs were relaxed and dangling from beneath its shell. Little light-green stripes adorned its legs, and she could see that it had claws, too. The turtle's head was stretched upward so that a ray of sunshine fell across him. He looked like he was in paradise.

So, this was Tena's friend. The turtle looked amazing as it sunned itself in the fresh air. To Sophie, it was truly an awesome sight. Being a city girl, the only animals she ever saw were in the zoo. Never anything like this.

Tena turned and whispered in her ear. "My friend is old. He will let you touch him if I ask him to." Sophie found it hard to believe that a wild reptile was going to let anyone touch it. She gave Tena a look of disbelief and would have laughed aloud if she had not been afraid it would scare the turtle away.

"You have to believe, or it will not work," Tena said rather sternly. "Do you want to touch him, or not?"

Sophie would not have believed that Tena could be cross for she seemed so good natured. It seemed, as though, Tena felt this was not something to be taken lightly.

Sophie grew serious and quickly replied, "I want to believe, I really do."

With that, Tena cautioned her, "Stay here until I call you."

Tena carefully stepped out around the tree. The turtle's head swung around quickly and his little black eyes were immediately focused on Tena.

"Well," thought Sophie, "so much for turtles acting slowly."

In a few seconds the turtle seemed to recognize her. Sophie watched with an open mouth as Tena walked deeper into the water until it was up to her waist. As she got closer, she heard Tena talking to the old turtle as if he were her long lost pal. Sophie was shocked at how calmly he looked at Tena.

Tena's voice was soothing and soft, and he seemed to be listening to her every word. Then Tena raised her arm and, to Sophie's amazement, reached out and touched the turtle's shell. She stroked the edge of the shell with her fingertips, and he seemed to like it. He closed his eyes just the way a cat does when you pet it.

Sophie was totally energized. This was better than hanging upside down on a roller coaster any day.

Tena was still talking to the turtle, but Sophie could not hear what she was saying. With her free hand, Tena motioned Sophie to come. Sophie's heart started beating faster and she was breathing rapidly. Was this wild creature actually going to let her get close? Did turtles bite?

Sophie wasn't waiting for any answers. She waded deeper. Now the cool water was almost up to her waist. She was so excited she could barely breathe. Tena whispered, "He says he will let you touch his shell."

"Awesome!" Sophie exclaimed, her eyes wide with wonder.

"Yes. But go slowly because he does not know you. And use only the soft part of your fingertips."

Barely breathing, Sophie moved her hand slowly until it was just barely touching the hard surface of the shell. The turtle raised his head slightly, but other than that he did not move.

The shell felt damp, but warm from the sunlight. His eyes

looked like little glass beads, and if a turtle could smile, Sophie was sure he would.

Tena spoke quietly. "I'm going to show you something else. My friend tells me he wants to swim over to another of his favorite spots. So, I asked him if you could tag along."

Before Sophie could say anything, Tena continued. "I will teach you how to do it, if you like."

"Well," Sophie thought to herself, "I just touched something wild. I guess I can learn something else new."

Tena went on, "I want you to pretend to be a turtle. Open your heart, and visualize traveling with his spirit as he swims to the other side of the pond."

Sophie thought this strange, to be sure. But why not try it?

Before she could ponder any further, Tena said, "Place your hand on your heart. Picture that your heart is filled with love. Think of someone you love a lot."

Sophie thought of her grandparents, one at a time, and then her mom and dad. At that point, everything shifted in her mind. She immediately thought of what had happened to her at the Parthenon when Athena nodded at her.

Just then the turtle slipped into the water and took off. Sophie imagined that she was going with him, plunging headfirst into the water. Her feet had webs between her toes that pushed through the water behind her, adding speed to her swimming.

She envisioned tiny black and silver fish darting around her in the water. Then, in her mind's eye, she saw the roots of the tree. She dove through the opening formed by the roots with such delight that her heart nearly burst from the thrill of it all. Next, she was pushing off the bottom of the stream. The round stones scattered as she headed for the surface, all the time holding her breath without the least bit of effort.

When Sophie broke free at the surface, she was herself again—in her own body, laughing out loud and breathing fast like she had run a race. "COOL! That was amazing! That was wild! I can't believe what just happened to me. I know it was my imagination, but it felt so real."

Tena gently took hold of her shoulder and they waded back to shore. They sat on two large rocks at the edge of the water to dry off and warm up.

Chapter 8

Sophie could not stop thinking about what had happened to her.

She realized she was shaking, but not from the cold. It was because she was overwhelmed. This was the most awesome experience she could ever have imagined.

The new friends sat by the water as it flowed past their feet. Wildflowers were growing nearby, and Tena asked Sophie if she had ever woven a wreath of flowers to wear on her head. Sophie had never done any such thing.

Tena pushed herself off the rock and led the way to where some flowers were growing. There were clover flowers—white and pink and purple—daisies in white and yellow, and some bright yellow ones with red tips on the petals. She showed Sophie how to pick them so they would have long stems. After collecting a handful of them, they came back to the rock to sit in the sun and dry out.

Tena taught Sophie how to braid the stems together, and before long a chain of flowers began to form. The chain grew longer and more colorful as they braided the stems together.

When enough flowers had been woven, Tena showed Sophie how to bend them together to make a crown of flowers. When they finished, the girls put them on their heads, laughing and giggling. Wearing the flower wreaths, they gazed down into the still water, admiring their reflection. Quite lovely, they decided.

Tena now began to walk back to the path, leaving behind the world of the stream. Sophie followed close behind.

They walked along through the fresh, green woods. The path was wide in this section, and the sun occasionally shone through to create patterns of light and dark on the ground. As Sophie looked around her, everything seemed to be brighter and richer in color than it had been on the way there.

She could hear birds singing, although she had not paid attention to them before. The air itself seemed alive, and a breeze gently lifted her hair off her shoulders. Sophie closed her eyes for a few moments to soak everything in.

She began to talk. "Tena, something's happening to me. Everything seems so different. I don't understand what's going on lately."

Tena smiled. "I think I might know. I'll tell you something my mother told me once. It may be a little hard to understand at first, but it's not anything terribly difficult. You're just seeing things in a different way, that's all."

Tena began by explaining that most people feel that they are alone and separated from everything on earth—often even from one another. "It doesn't matter whether we're talking about people or animals or trees or rocks. Everyone thinks that everything in the world exists separately from everything else. It's seen as being the normal way. I've learned that feeling separated from everyone and everything is not the normal way of things."

Tena went on to say that people in the past had always lived close to the earth and understood the ways of nature. "The truth is we are all connected to one another, and to nature, too. We just don't know it."

"What happened to you back there was that for a brief moment, just a couple of minutes, you were not separate from that turtle. You were connected to him, weren't you?"

"I'll say I was," Sophie said. "I felt like I was flying through that water. It was so neat. I never thought anything like that was possible. So, tell me more."

"I have a question for you first, Sophie," Tena said. "If I asked you to guess what connects you to your family, what would you tell me?"

Sophie thought for a minute. "I think love is like glue and that's what holds us together."

"True!" Tena agreed. "Love is the most amazing power in the world, don't you think?"

"Well," Sophie added, "sometimes it seems like there is a lot of bad news on television. I watch CNN with my dad once in a while."

Tena turned around and walked backwards. "My mother told me that anger and hatred are based on ignorance. This is when people don't understand the power of love. What do you think?"

Sophie pondered for a moment. "Well, you could be right. When you love people, if they say or do stupid things, you forgive them even if they upset you."

"Exactly!" Tena answered back.

Sophie said, "So, with the turtle back there you told me to think of love and to open my heart. Why did you say that?"

"Because," Tena replied, "love comes from your heart. An open heart is a heart that can feel and know things that you would otherwise miss."

"You know, Tena, I've had some interesting things happen to me like this open-heart stuff."

Tena stopped walking backwards, turned around, and fell in beside Sophie. "Tell me about them," she said.

Sophie told her about the last day of school and how when she was texting her friends she had experienced an unusual feeling in her heart of love for her friends. She also told her about the decision to come on the trip, even though she knew it would mean not being with her friends during the summer. She had *felt* somewhere inside herself that she was supposed to come to Greece.

Then, Sophie told her about the Parthenon and the Goddess Athena and what had happened. She included every detail she could remember about what she had seen and the look the goddess had given her. She talked about how she had thought of love and the Parthenon daydream when they had been back there in the water. And then how she swam with the turtle. When she finally finished, she had talked so fast she was breathless.

Tena explained, "An open heart makes you feel things you might miss. My mother has always said that when you trust your feelings—she calls that intuition—you find your wisdom. Just like the day you decided to come to Greece and meet me," she declared, laughing now.

"Intuition?" Sophie pondered. "Do you think that's what I was feeling?"

"Oh, yes, Sophie." Tena responded. "You're just beginning to know what intuition can do."

Here the path opened into a clearing, and at the bottom of the hill they could see a group of houses and other buildings. Pointing to a pale green house, Tena announced, "That's my house. Let's race to see who can get there first."

In an instant, they were running and laughing. "It was turning out to be an exceptionally good day after all," Sophie thought, as she skipped over the road ahead.

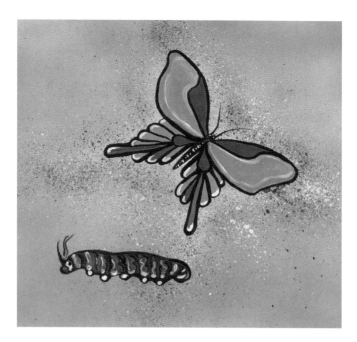

Chapter 9
The Magic Loom

Tena's house was on the outer edge of what looked to be the beginning of a small village. The houses in Greece were different from what Sophie was used to. Tena's house was a single-story house with a red tile roof. It was painted light green, and as they drew closer she saw that a large sign had been painted right on the corner wall of the house. It was an image of a woman weaving on a loom. Around the circular picture there was writing in Greek and English that read: *The Magic Loom*. Tena informed her that this was the name of her family's business.

The girls walked around the side of the house where a door was standing open. Tena told Sophie that her mother, Métis, did not know much English, so she would translate their conversations.

With enthusiasm, Tena's mom, Métis, burst out of the house. "Ella Mesa! Ella Mesa! – Come in! Come in!" She grabbed Sophie's hands and shook them with delight. Then in broken English, she blurted out, "Come with me. Eat. Eat now, with us."

Chapter 9

Tena was laughing, talking to her mother in Greek. She turned to Sophie. "I don't think I have to translate that. But in case you did not get what she meant, she's inviting you to have lunch with us."

They walked around to the back of the house where there was a patio with a red tile roof and a large table set for a meal. Sophie was fascinated that in Greece people loved to sit and eat outside much more than her family ever did.

Tena's mother motioned to them to sit down, and soon food was being brought out of the house. Plates of pita bread, cheese, melon, and grapes appeared. Métis put shish kebobs of lamb and vegetables on a small grill nearby. Of course, there was a bowl of kalamata olives on the table. They were a little too close to Sophie, who scrunched up her nose in disproval. When no one was looking, she moved the bowl of olives to the other side of the table.

Tena's mother looked young. She had brown hair streaked by the sun and hazel green eyes that flashed. She had a thin face and large nose, as did most of the people Sophie had met so far. It made her uncomfortable because she was so self-conscious about her own nose. Yet, Métis looked absolutely lovely. She wore a white dress with lace on the sleeves and was barefoot.

Tena's mother prepared the food and Tena helped serve it. She came and sat next to Sophie.

"I've noticed that everyone here loves to eat," Sophie said.

Tena laughed. "Yes, we welcome our guests with food. It is the Greek way. We talk with our hands, we hug, we kiss, and we love to dance. These are my people, and it has been this way forever."

They ate until Sophie regretted it, and when Tena's mother offered her more food, she had to protest and say, "No more, please."

One thing Sophie noticed was that Métis had the most graceful hands she had ever seen. The way she moved her hands reminded Sophie of music, of running water in the stream, of flowers bending in the wind. They literally floated and tipped and fluttered through space.

When they finally had finished eating and put everything away, Métis said, "Come, see my weavings."

She led the way into a large room that was open on three sides. The room was situated so that you looked out on the countryside below. You could see a vineyard on one side and a meadow on the other. There was a mountain in the background, all dusty purple against the perpetually blue sky.

It was a wonderful place to work because the breeze blew right through the area. If it rained, large canvas curtains could be tied across the openings to protect the several large wooden-framed weaving machines placed around the room.

Métis called Sophie over to one of the looms where she had been working. It was incredible to see, for it had countless threads hooked to the back and sides. Sophie knew something of weaving because her other grandmother was Navajo, and they had rugs belonging to her in almost every room of their home. Yet, she could not remember much about the technique of weaving because she had been so small when she had visited her grandmother.

Métis took her to a wall of many skeins of wool in different colors. There was every color of the rainbow and then some. She explained that they dyed the wool themselves with natural ingredients. Sophie got out her camera and took some pictures.

Métis sat down at her loom and began to weave. She effortlessly pulled a thread across the length of the bar. She stepped on a foot pedal that set the thread firmly in place and created room for the next thread. Back and forth she wove the colored thread that was connected to a wooden shuttle. Her hands moved gracefully, gaining speed as she went. Sophie was amazed at how fast she worked and how much she wove in just a few minutes.

Then Métis got up and urged Sophie, "Try." Sophie sat down and tried to remember what to do. It was a lot harder than it looked when she was watching Métis weave. After some difficulty, she finally managed to get the thread across and used the foot peddle to pull it into place.

She looked over at Tena and asked, "Can you weave, too?"

"Oh, yes." Tena answered. "I've been weaving since I was six. When I started, I, too, had difficulty, the same as anyone trying to learn something new."

Métis walked away and disappeared into a back room. She quickly reappeared with a large rolled bundle in her arms. "Come! Come!" she motioned. On a large table she unrolled the bundle and spread out the weavings.

The first was a brilliantly colored rug or tapestry with a geometric design created by using diamond shapes in many colors. The diamonds were layered in such a way that the piece looked like it was three-dimensional. Sophie realized that some of the patterns were similar to Native American patterns used by her grandmother.

The next weaving had a field of flowers in warm colors of red and orange on a field of green. With each cloth you could see the artistry involved. Tena explained that her mother had won national recognition for weaving tapestries that looked incredibly real.

Another weaving depicted a statue of the Goddess Aphrodite emerging from the sea. She was beautiful, and Sophie thought it looked like a painting. She knew, though, that the image had actually been woven into the fabric one thread at a time. It was hard to imagine how anyone could create something so beautiful.

Métis asked, "You like?"

Sophie responded, "Yes, I like it very much." Métis smiled broadly and patted Sophie's back.

"Please, wait," she said and went back into the workroom. She returned holding a small bundle in her hands. She opened the bundle and placed it on the table. When Sophie saw it, she gasped.

The tapestry depicted a bright blue butterfly woven with metallic threads. The piece was not large, but perfect for Sophie to hold in her hands. Sophie could not help but pick it up and watch its threads reflect in the soft sunlight. There were several shades of blue in the tapestry, and the more she stared, the more the butterfly looked like it was moving.

Sophie placed the piece back on the table, but Métis picked the tapestry up and pressed it into her hands. In English she said, "You! You, Sophie!" Sophie had a puzzled look on her face. She didn't quite understand.

Tena explained, "She wants to give it to you. It is a gift."

But Sophie felt that she couldn't accept it. "Oh, I can't take this. It is too valuable to give as a gift."

She would have protested further, but Tena said, "If you do not take it, my mother will have her feelings hurt."

Sophie stopped her protest and looked at the tapestry again. It was rich in color, and actually looked real. "Tell your mother that I love the gift and will treasure it forever." She clutched the tapestry to her heart and held it there with her eyes closed—feeling the love that Tena's mother had woven into it. It felt rich and beautiful.

Métis spoke rapidly in Greek. Tena translated for Sophie, "When I created it, I knew it was for someone special. I didn't know who that might be, but as soon as I saw you, I knew it belonged to you." Continuing, with Tena translating, she asked, "Do you know the meaning of the butterfly?

"Please, tell me," Sophie begged.

Tena translated as Métis explained. "We all start out in life like a caterpillar, a little worm crawling on the ground. We think that our world is large and that the events around us are important. We think about eating and sleeping and trying to stay safe, and not much else occupies our mind."

"Then one day we start to feel that something is changing within us. Of course, we do not know what that is. Our skin feels strange. Our bodies no longer feel like they fit. We struggle with trying to be happy crawling on the ground, where before we had been happy. We find ourselves building a cocoon, not understanding why or even what it is. While we are in the cocoon, we undergo a complete metamorphosis."

"The day we emerge, we look around and don't understand who we are because we have changed so much. Oh, what a remarkable day it is when we discover the wings on our back, and realize we can take off and fly."

"Only at that moment do we understand just how small our world was before. Our wings can take us to new heights, and our bodies are ready to live a new kind of life."

"This is your journey right now, Sophie. You were a baby once, then a little girl, and soon you will become a woman. Don't be unhappy with your life as it is right now. Don't be unhappy with your body or anything else you see changing around you."

"I want you to know that you will discover the power of dreaming. Do not settle for limitations in your life. You are a butterfly now, Sophie, and you can fly."

Sophie was deeply moved by Métis' gift and her wise words. Sophie thanked Tena's mother again and told her that whenever she looked at the weaving, she would try to remember to dream of being a butterfly, but she wasn't completely sure she understood its meaning.

Métis laughed and patted her shoulder saying, "Good, Sophie! Good." She folded up the tapestry and put it in a plain cloth bag so Sophie could take it with her.

A feeling of warmth moved back and forth between the three of them until they began to giggle.

Next, Métis gave a small container of fresh olives to Sophie. She said in English, "Take. Eat!" Tena began to laugh because she had seen the look on Sophie's face when she moved the olives to the other side of the table at lunch.

Tena translated for Métis, "I noticed you didn't eat many olives at lunch, so please take them home." Tena was biting her lip, trying not to laugh out loud.

Sophie held out her hand and politely thanked Métis, reluctantly putting the container into her backpack. She knew she did not want to offend her hostess by refusing them.

By this time they realized it was time to leave if Sophie was going to get home by six o'clock. Métis gave Sophie a strong hug. Sophie promised to come again, and the two girls set off for the woods.

Tena explained that she did not want Sophie to get lost, so she was planning to walk with her as far as the Sweetheart Trees. Sophie should have no problem walking the rest of the way by herself from there.

The two girls walked together, feeling comfortable with each other. They had started this day as strangers, and now they were friends.

When they reached the Sweetheart Trees, Sophie looked down the path and could see the Blue House from where she stood. Tena turned to her and became serious.

She paused before she spoke, as if she were thinking something over. "Tomorrow I want to take you to my secret place. You cannot tell anyone where we're going. Can you keep a secret?"

Sophie's eyes grew large. "Yes, I can keep a secret."

"Good," Tena said. "I will meet you tomorrow in this spot around eight o'clock in the morning. Do not worry if I'm a little late, because I will be coming. I'm going to show you something I think you've never seen before."

Sophie asked, "Like the turtle?" She did not want to part without knowing something about the secret.

"Even better," Tena replied.

Sophie had taught Tena how to give a high-five, so they smacked hands high in the air. Sophie had to jump a little higher, since she was much shorter than Tena. With that, Tena started back down the path, waving goodbye.

As Sophie walked on toward the Blue House, she thought about her day. That morning she felt lonely and was upset because she was missing out on the fun with her friends. She felt far away from everyone and was feeling pretty homesick. Now, it seemed like she was a completely different person.

She held her head high and stood a little straighter. Maybe she could become a butterfly after all.

Chapter 10

The Secret

When Sophie got closer to the Blue House, she saw the van Nikos always drove parked outside the back door. It was late afternoon, so Sophie was surprised to find Nikos sitting at the kitchen table talking to Nina when she went inside. The two greeted her enthusiastically.

Nikos said, "Sophie, your grandfather sent me up here to bring you back to the site. Today, we began to unearth the statue, and she is a beauty." He explained that they had decided to work until the statue was totally uncovered, even if that meant that they worked all night. "Everyone knew you would want to be there. Right?"

"Sure I do," Sophie answered. "Just let me take something to my room and I'll be right down."

"No problem," Nikos said.

Sophie hurried upstairs and pulled out her tapestry of the butterfly. She unfolded it and laid it out on the bed. It looked even more beautiful, if that was possible. She lovingly touched it and then went to the computer to send her parents a quick message.

Chapter 10

Hello to you both! I feel totally different than I did this morning. I had a wonderful time with my new friend, Tena. Can't wait to tell you about it. I'm going to the site today to unearth the second statue. Will send photos in the morning. Sweet dreams to you both! Sophie.

And with that, she sent the message.

She flew downstairs, put a cold bottle of soda in her backpack, and hurried over to where Nikos stood waiting to take her to the site. Nina said goodnight, since her husband was coming to get her soon. Sophie thanked her again for introducing her to Tena, and suddenly realized as she stood there that of all the people she had hugged in the past two weeks, she had never hugged Nina. She impulsively gave Nina a big hug, causing her to smile from ear to ear. And her dark eyes grew moist and shiny.

After Sophie climbed into the van, Nikos drove with the same skill he had used in Athens. Driving on both sides of the road to avoid the numerous potholes, they bounced their way to the site. When they arrived they went to the area that was lit up. Although it was still light out, it would soon be dark. The gasoline generator was already running to supply electricity to the lights that were now aimed at the sculpture that was being uncovered.

Before Sophie could get a good look, her grandfather came roaring up, all animated. He had dirt on his hands and knees, and was absolutely on fire with excitement. "I created the perfect spot for you, kiddo," he said, leading her over to a canvas chair that looked like it had survived a war. It looked sturdy enough, so she swung herself onto the seat.

"You bring your camera?" he asked.

"Yes," she replied, beginning to pull it out of her backpack.

"I want you to document what we are doing," he told her. "Take this seriously, even though one of the students will also be taking pictures. He will be doing something else with his photos. Kiddo, take as many pictures as you like, just be careful not to get in anyone's way. I have to go over there now and help."

She reached out and caught her grandfather's arm as she looked to the statue being unearthed. "Who is she?"

"Artemis," he said, pointing to the statue's head. "See that crown she is wearing? It has a crescent moon on it. That has to mean Artemis." He left her and walked to where he had been working.

The Secret

Everyone was there. The graduate students were working on the statue. A canvas had been set up to collect the dirt and sand as it was worked away from the surface of the figure. Earth still encased the statue up to her elbows, but her face and upper body were wonderful to see.

When Diane saw Sophie she gave her a wink of recognition. She had a trowel, a common small excavation tool, and was carefully probing and pulling dirt away from the right side of the body where a hand and arm should be. Robert was working on the other side. Both were concentrating and moved slowly and carefully. The excitement was so strong it seemed to have a life of its own.

The earth yielded easily and soon Artemis' elbow was showing. She outstretched her hands—again carved in a gesture of welcome. Sophie's grandmother was working on the back of the sculpture, using a fine brush to remove all the grains of sand. Layers of dirt were smoothly carried away and fresh canvas gathered more debris.

Sophie, no longer on her chair, moved quickly around them with her camera. Looking. Clicking the camera. Moving in and out. Soon the statue's arms were uncovered, and then they were at her waist. Someone remarked that things were going fast because the goddess was eager to come out of hiding.

Now her knees could be seen and she was wearing a short tunic. The folds of the tunic showed movement like she had just been running. As Sophie walked around to the back of the statue she saw that Artemis had a quiver of arrows over her shoulder. She noticed that the sculptor had carved each arrow flawlessly. Her hand held a bow that balanced on the pedestal. Her legs indicated motion, as if she had run over to this spot and stopped.

Hours passed, but it felt like only minutes. When the last bit of earth was brushed from the surface, Artemis stood gracefully in her place. In that moment, as everyone said later, it was as if time stood still and the Ancients were right there with them.

At that moment, a rushing wind arose and blew through the camp. The trees bent and the leaves made such an intense noise of motion that it was like a storm had been released. Two male students grabbed the lights to keep them from tipping over, and dusty dirt blew out from the area in all directions.

Chapter 10

It continued for a number of minutes, and Sophie was overcome with a feeling that was eerie and exciting all at the same time.

"Artemis, is that you?" she asked. "Are you here? Are you happy to be free?" Sophie had said this aloud, but no one could hear her over the noise of the wind and the leaves in the trees.

Then, just like that, it was over. No rain, no storm, nothing. Everyone just stared silently at one another. There was a curious feeling in the air and it stayed there for a long time.

Sophie thought to herself, "Artemis is celebrating. She is back."

It seemed to Sophie that no one wanted to leave. It was like going to a party where everyone was having so much fun that it was hard to say goodnight. Professor Conrad, who had overseen the excavation, suddenly looked tired. He asked the workmen to put up a large walk-in tent. Several students were going to stay and sleep on the site with him. They feared that someone could come and steal the statues. Looters were paid a lot of money for stolen artwork, and the professor was not taking any chances.

Sophie's grandparents were slowing down, too, so Nikos drove the three of them back to the house. In the commotion, Sophie had forgotten to eat. So, she thanked everyone for letting her be a part of something so spectacular, and she grabbed an apple and headed for bed.

In the morning, Sophie was surprised to discover that her grandparents were still in the house, as they usually left at dawn. They were eating breakfast when Sophie came into the kitchen. Nina was not coming in until noon today, so her grandmother made pancakes for her, and they began talking.

Her grandfather told her they had tested the earth and now knew there were more statues. "Very cool," thought Sophie, as she poured more syrup on her pancakes.

When she finished eating, she announced, "I have something to show you. Wait here." She brought the tapestry down and placed it on the table. Her grandparents were speechless as they stared at it.

Her grandmother finally spoke. "Honey, where did you get this?"

Sophie told them all about Tena and her mother and the loom and the gift. By then her grandparents were touching the weaving and looking at it from front to back in amazement. "This is exceptionally fine work. What is Tena's mother's name?" her grandmother asked. Sophie replied, "Métis." Her grandmother commented that the name sounded familiar, but she did not think she knew her.

Sophie told them about the meaning of the butterfly, but was not going to share anything else—at least, not yet. Who knew how they might react to her wading in a stream and touching a wild turtle. Sophie was not ready to take the risk that they might not understand all that she was learning about herself.

So, she simply explained that she was meeting her friend, Tena, again today and that she had to get ready. With that, she left them in the kitchen and went back upstairs.

Sophie left the Blue House in plenty of time to be at the Sweetheart Trees by eight o'clock. She walked barefoot in the shallows of the stream. She looked for the turtle, but he was not there. So she sat down on a rock and waited for Tena to come, thinking all the while about the statue of Artemis.

Tena softly called out to her when she arrived. Sophie went over and they did their special high-five, making their hands smack loudly, which was part of the fun. Tena led the way and Sophie fell in beside her.

"What can you tell me about Artemis?" Sophie asked.

"Well, for one thing, she was independent and brave," Tena said. "When she was our age, she went to her father, Zeus, and asked him if she could leave the beautiful palace where all the gods and goddesses lived and go live in the woods."

Sophie laughed, "I bet that went over big."

Tena laughed, too. "It did not please her father at all. You see, in those days, the whole of Greece was covered with forests that were filled with wild animals—like bears and wolves. Her father couldn't understand why anyone would want to live in those dangerous woods. So, he told Artemis, no."

"Artemis was not to be put off. She wanted to be free and live as she pleased. Finally, her father realized that he couldn't stop her and gave her his blessing, even though he didn't understand her feelings."

"What else should I know about her?" Sophie asked.

"Well, she protected children and women, as well as animals. She loved nature and understood all its secrets."

Sophie told Tena about unearthing the Artemis statue the night before, and how the wind had blown and how magnificent the statue was. Tena listened with obvious interest to what Sophie was telling her.

About that time they came to the edge of the path, the same place they had stood yesterday. Tena turned to Sophie. "I'm going to show you my secret place, but you must promise me again that you will never tell anyone."

Sophie did not flinch a bit. She immediately held up her hand and declared loudly and clearly, "I promise never to tell anyone...not EVER!"

"Okay, then," Tena said. "Follow me. And walk where I walk, move where I move, and do not say a word until I tell you it is safe to talk, okay?"

Tena looked carefully in both directions and waited until she was absolutely sure they were alone. "We must go off this path," she whispered. "Let's go. Just follow me."

In front of them were tall bushes and rocks and trees—and no path at all. As Tena walked, she chose first one rock and then another to walk on. As Sophie followed, she slipped between the bushes and tall grass, and before she knew it she was on the other side of a wall of green.

The area they had just entered looked just as thick and hard to see through as it had on the other side. There was a different feeling on this side of the wall. It felt quiet and calm here, although the sun seemed not as bright as on the other side.

Tena moved even farther away from the wall. "Now we can talk without anyone on the other path hearing us." She pointed to the ground. "Look! See the stones?"

"Yes." Sophie could see them. They were broken stones that she guessed had once been a road.

"It is left over from olden times," Tena explained. "If we follow this road, it will take us to the secret place I want you to see."

Now, the girls entered an emerald green world. It was much cooler and Sophie wished she had brought a sweater. The light was definitely different. Everything looked richer in color, like after a rain, but the ground was not wet.

They followed the winding uneven path created by the stones, all the time going deeper and deeper into the woods. Sophie felt uneasy and she jumped when she heard a strange bird's cry. She stopped and tugged on Tena's arm. "What's that?"

"Don't worry," Tena assured her. "That's just the sound of an owl. There are many owls in the woods, and besides, she is probably just hunting for breakfast."

"*Breakfast* is not going to be me, right?" Sophie asked.

Tena, who had seemed more serious since they had come into this part of the forest, said, "No!" She laughed a little and then added, "You have nothing to worry about."

Finally, they came to a hill where the stony road stopped. Tena grabbed Sophie's wrist and pointed. "Up there." They left the stones and climbed up the steep side to the top of the hill. Then Tena said, "Look!"

Sophie did and was not disappointed. Before her was an astounding scene—one she would remember for the rest of her life. There stood the largest, most grand tree she had ever seen. Its trunk was as wide as a small house. Its branches went twisting and turning upward toward the heavens. The canopy of thousands upon thousands of leaves shimmered in the sunlight. It looked like it was lit up from inside.

Sophie was not aware that she was walking toward the tree. No, it would be more accurate to say that she was running toward the tree.

It was as if an invisible magnet drew her. She could not stop herself.

As she drew closer, the tree filled her entire view. She could see nothing but the tree. She remembered Tena and turned to see where she was. Tena had been running right behind her and was standing close by.

"Tena, how old is this tree?" she asked.

"Old, very old," Tena told her. "Some say it is thousands of years old. Some say it was here when the Ancients lived here. They say it is a *living being* that has witnessed many things and has survived through time. She is definitely old."

Before seeing this tree, Sophie would not have thought of a tree as a person. Yet, it was clear that this tree was like no other she had ever seen. Yes, she was alive. Both girls just stared and walked back and forth, looking at the tree. They laughed at her huge body and wondered at her mighty branches.

Finally, Sophie walked back a short way and sat down. She just didn't know what to say. The tree was so impressive and powerful to look at. Tena sat down beside Sophie and finally broke the silence. "There is more about this tree that I want to tell you."

"Really?" Sophie replied, excitedly. "What do you mean?"

Tena continued. "There is a legend about this tree—a story that I have heard since I was a little girl."

"What is it?" Sophie asked.

Tena leaned back and began to tell the story. "Well, it is said that this was once a sacred grove of trees. These trees were blessed by the Goddess of Nature, Artemis. People believed she walked in these woods."

"There were many goddess temples in this area, including the one your grandparents are exploring. These temples were meticulously built and contained many treasures and statues made by the finest artisans of the day. Some believe that this forest covers some of these temples, and that many wonders are still hidden under the ground."

"As the story goes, one night Iris, a high Priestess who oversaw all the temples, was told that a band of fierce warriors planned to steal the precious golden objects in the temples. However, the Priestess learned that it was not just the gold they were after, but a statue that possessed magical powers in one particular temple."

"According to the story, Priestess Iris gathered together all the people who lived in the nearby village and asked them to help her hide the temples' treasures. After all the treasures were concealed, the people hid in caves and secluded corners of the woods."

"It is said that Iris set for herself the task of hiding the magical statue that the warriors wanted to steal. It stood in an open plaka so all could see it. On her head was a golden crown of stars. It was an *Oracle*-statue and it was believed to possess wisdom."

Sophie interrupted. "What's an Oracle-statue?"

"Oh!" Tena responded. "Think of the statue as a house that the goddess spirit lives in. When the Priestess needed wisdom to help her people, she would go to the statue and ask the spirit for advice."

Sophie's mouth fell open. "This is like just the Parthenon where the Goddess Athena lived in her colossal statue!"

"You're exactly right," Tena agreed.

"Okay," Sophie said, "please tell me more, continue." She wrapped her arms around her knees and listened with her whole body.

"Well, the Priestess was determined not to let the statue of the Goddess of Wisdom fall into the warriors' hands. She devised a special plan to save it. She took an artist's chisel and broke the body of the statue into several pieces. First, she cut off the head, then the arms, next the legs, and finally the torso. Second, she set out to hide the pieces of the statue and told no one where they were hidden."

"So, the warriors came and found an empty temple. Everything of value was tucked away. The Oracle was gone. The villagers were gone. Since there was nothing to steal, they left."

"Once the warriors were gone, the villagers returned from their hiding places one by one, bringing with them the sacred objects they had hidden. That is, they brought everything except the statue that the Priestess had been responsible for protecting."

"The legend says that Iris hid the head of the statue in a big tree and the other parts of the statue's body in different places. When she went to find the tree where she had hidden the head, she searched and searched and searched, but could not find it. Nor could she find any of her other hiding places. Iris was devastated. She wailed. She tore at her hair and fell on her knees, begging the goddess to show her where the pieces were hidden."

"One night Artemis appeared to Iris as she was wandering through the forest searching for the pieces of the statue."

Sophie couldn't help herself. "What did Artemis do?" she asked anxiously.

"She told Iris not to be concerned, that the statue was safe, and that she had done a brave and noble thing. Artemis proclaimed that from then on she would protect the statue until the day the right person would find her."

"Artemis then told Iris that she was bestowing the power of the Oracle upon her and that she would become a living Oracle filled with wisdom to guide her people. She would then be able to teach other women to be Oracles. That knowledge was handed down until Delphi was destroyed."

Tena continued the story. "Of course, the exquisite statue's head rested safely in the tree, never to be found. The tree grew around the head, until finally the tree and the statue became one."

Chapter 10

Sophie had been listening with rapt attention to Tena as she told the story. Then Sophie asked in a whisper, "Is this the same tree?"

Tena replied, "Yes, it is."

Sophie looked again at the tree and asked, "Where is it? The statue's head, I mean. Where is it?"

Tena stood up slowly and reached down to help Sophie get to her feet. She led her around to the other side of the tree. There, in the middle of the body of the tree was a natural opening.

Sophie asked with mounting curiosity, "Can you still see it, the statue's head?"

"Yes, it's still a part of the tree," Tena said.

Tena motioned for Sophie to follow her. She held out her hand and helped Sophie up onto the first large root extending from the tree's base. Sophie continued to climb up the roots, one after the other, balancing herself, and holding onto the side of the tree.

"If you stand exactly where you are, you can easily see into the opening," Tena advised.

Sophie asked, "Will I see *her*?"

"Yes," said Tena. "She is there. After all this time she is still there, inside the tree."

Sophie was careful not to fall, using both hands to hold on and peer inside. "I don't see anything," she stated with disappointment.

"Keep looking," Tena advised. "At first, it is just too dark. Let your eyes adjust, and you will be able to see it."

Sophie continued to look inside the tree. Her heart was beating faster as she peered into the darkness. Slowly—very slowly—her eyes adjusted to the dark interior of the tree. She thought she saw something just in front of her. "What was that?"

The more she gazed, the clearer it became. A white marble face was looking at her. The face looked serene.

As Sophie gawked at the face, she felt as if she were looking at a real live goddess. A feeling of concern moved outwardly from her heart. She found herself wishing that she could find all the parts of the statue and put them together again. Without thinking, she reached in and gently stroked the cheek of the lovely face.

She heard Tena gasp, "Did you touch her?"

"Yes." Sophie turned to tell her she had. "Why? Wasn't it alright to do so?"

"I don't know," Tena admitted. She was standing below, staring up at Sophie with a look of surprise on her face.

Sophie then made her way back down the roots of the tree. They both walked over to the grassy edge and sat down in silence.

Finally, Sophie spoke. "This is a mysterious place. Did you say people still look for the statue?"

"Yes." Tena said. "They do. I'm sure that if they ever found it, they would tear open the tree to get to it."

Sophie cringed with disgust. "Oh! That would surely kill the tree."

"Oh, yes." Tena agreed. "I feel sure it would."

"You are right, Tena, to keep this place a secret. We cannot tell anyone about this tree."

The girls hugged to seal the pact. They would not talk of this tree to anyone except each other. It would be their secret.

Finally, they got up and began walking back to the secret wall in the woods, following the crumbled stony road just like they had done to get to the tree.

They had not gone far when both girls slowed their pace, looked back over their shoulders at the tree. Sophie felt that she had found a rare treasure.

At the green wall, Tena led the way as before, and Sophie followed her out of the thicket. Sophie looked at her watch and saw that it was now early afternoon. She invited Tena to come to the Blue House with her to eat and then go to the excavation site.

Tena explained, "I want to see the site, but my mother is going to be taking our tapestries to town to ship to our customers. She needs my help in packing them this afternoon. Tomorrow we will both take the bus to the city where we can ship things. I will be gone all day."

"Well, let's get together in two days," Sophie suggested.

Tena smiled. "Great! You can take me to the ruins that day. I would like that."

"Okay," Sophie said. "Cool!"

They gave each other a farewell hug and headed for home. As Sophie walked toward the Blue House, the tree and the statue's lovely face danced in her thoughts.

Chapter 11
The Dream

Sophie was lying in bed in her favorite summer nightgown. It was purple accented with little yellow stars. She had propped herself up on her pillows and was reflecting on her day. Seeing the tree had been an intense experience, and the face of the statue inside it was still in her thoughts.

She had gone to the site shortly after getting back to the house. The graduate students had cleared away a wide sweep of earth, so that the uncovered statues stood with about twenty feet or more of empty space in front of them. They had discovered that the columns and the two statues already excavated were connected to a base on the floor of the temple that formed a semi-circle.

The team believed, based on the measurements they had taken, that there had to be more statues, and they had located where the next two would be. The area in front of the statues concealed a floor of mosaic patterns, and to remove all the dirt might cause damage to the floor, so it remained covered.

Chapter 11

Tomorrow the crew was going to begin working on both uncovered statues at the same time, so the entire team gathered downstairs at the house to plan how they were going to make it happen. The whole group was excited about what they might find since they had uncovered another mystery just before they had stopped work for the day. On the area in front of the statues, they had found the remains of a small pedestal. It looked like a statue had once stood on it, but nothing was there now.

If you had come upon the temple in the past, you would have seen this statue first and then the other statues behind it, forming a crescent. It puzzled everyone, because if all the other statues had been buried with the idea that they were to be found in the future, like Sophie's time capsule idea, then why was this statue missing?

It looked like it had been cut or broken off of its pedestal. None of the pieces of the missing statue had been found, and this just added to the 'what-could-it-possibly-mean' feeling that was running through everyone's mind.

Sophie was thinking of the story that Tena had told her earlier today. She remembered how Tena said that the Priestess Iris had hidden the statue in several places piece by piece. Sophie had seen the head of what probably was the statue missing from the archaeological site where her grandparents were working. It seemed almost impossible that she knew a part of the story that no one else knew.

The professor had hired men to guard the site at night, and he was also sleeping there to make sure nothing happened to the artifacts they were finding. Sophie had excused herself from the activity downstairs early, saying that she was tired. She had wanted to e-mail her friends and her parents a picture of the blue butterfly tapestry. The weaving hung on her wall, carefully tacked up so she could see it the first thing in the morning when she woke up and the last thing at night when she went to bed.

Soon, Sophie realized she was getting sleepy. She slid down and stretched out on top of her covers. The moon was full and filled up her entire bedroom. The tapestry's metallic threads glittered in the light. Sophie's eyes were open, but she thought to herself, "I think I'm asleep and I'm dreaming." As she looked at the blue butterfly shining in the moonlight, she thought that something was moving inside the tapestry.

She leaned forward and sure enough it was like something was struggling to be released. Then an actual blue butterfly pushed its wings out of the cloth and broke free. It fluttered around the room slowly. It glided, more than fluttered, over her head toward the window. Sophie watched in amazement and thought, "I hope it doesn't leave without me." Instead, the butterfly just hovered, turning to look at her.

Sophie was thinking that this was a nice dream. She sat up on the edge of her bed. She stood up and walked to the window. The butterfly unexpectedly landed on her head. It just sat there exercising its wings, gently moving them back and forth.

Quickly, it flew around her head and out the window a foot or so above the windowsill. Sophie reached to catch it and tilted forward. As she did this, for just a second, both of her feet left the floor. She struggled to plant them back on the floor. Had she just become weightless? Had she actually flown?

It had been a long time since she had experienced a flying dream. She used to have them all the time when she was a little girl. Now, she was having one again. "Well, okay," she thought, "I love to fly."

Next, she jumped upward to help get off the ground. It worked, because she was now floating about a foot off the floor. The blue butterfly got excited and flew around in a little circle. Then it hovered just out of reach.

"Oh! This is s-o-o-o cool!" She tested things out, willing herself to climb higher and to be able to turn. She lifted her right arm and shoulder, and effortlessly turned to the right. "Wow!" She made a circle around the bed while looking at her arms that were now glowing silver from the moonlight. She laughed aloud. It was such an awesome feeling to be flying, to be weightless. Of course, she knew she was dreaming, but it was nonetheless an awe-inspiring moment.

"Well, let's go for it." Sophie tilted forward and glided out the window. Flying just a short distance from her head, watching what she was doing, the butterfly acted as her guide. It began to fly forward, and she willingly followed. Below her was the garden of the Blue House, the clothesline, and the tool shed.

Sophie flew on, not minding that she was high above the ground. After all, it was only a dream. There was no real reason to be afraid of falling.

Chapter 11

The butterfly led her over the forest behind the house, climbing upward so she would clear the trees. She called out to the butterfly to wait up while she sailed around a bit just to take a look at things. The house was very blue in the moonlight. Downstairs where the lights were on, everything was golden in color, with voices and laughter flowing out into the night. It seemed everyone was eating and was quite excited about whatever plans they were making.

The upper part of the house was quiet, her bedroom window still open. She could see the road, all dusty and quiet, with Nikos's van parked in the driveway. After drinking in the sights around the Blue House, she turned and continued on her flying adventure.

The butterfly fluttered over the tree line, and from time to time she could see the stream below gleaming in the moonlight. Like a ribbon of silver, it peeked out between the treetops, and she wondered if turtles slept at night or played with the reflection of the moon in the water.

The night was alive, the sky a deep violet and the full moon majestic. She heard birds and insects, and she thought she saw an owl flying far below her, hunting for something in the night. Later, when she looked over her shoulder, she could not see the house anymore.

But she did not care. She was having too much fun soaring, to worry about it. She wondered where the butterfly was taking her, since it seemed to know where it was going.

Then she reached a place in the forest that she recognized. The tree below them was the one Tena and she visited earlier. The butterfly made a wide slow circle around the tree, and she followed its example. She saw a radiant light below her, at what she guessed was likely to be the base of tree. The effect was as if the light were shining up through the leaves of the tree itself. It created a glow making the tree look alive, like a candle in the night.

It was then that the butterfly started descending. Sophie, for the first time, felt a little apprehensive, although she did not know why. She did not like nightmares, and she hoped this was not going to be one. She wondered why the butterfly brought her here.

Once she broke through the cover of the leaves and floated down to the ground, she had no fear at all. Everything had a warm, buttery light around it, and it was not dark or spooky. She wished Tena was here to see this. She vowed to remember everything, so she could at least tell her about it.

Sophie's bare feet felt damp as they touched the cool grass. There was a nice flat rock in the grass, and she thought this would make a delightful seat. She sat down on it as if she were waiting for something, although what she was waiting for, she could not say.

In dreams, time does not work the same as in real life. So how long she sat there and waited she did not know. She did have a sense that she was waiting for something or someone, and the blue butterfly hovered just a few feet from her shoulder, as if to keep her company while she waited.

Gradually, the forest grew quiet. The crickets and birds stopped singing. It seemed like all life was holding its breath, and she, too, was holding her breath.

Next, she realized the light was actually pouring out of an opening in the tree and seemed to take the form of two hands. They were translucent, clear, and golden, and the long fingers wrapped themselves around the edges of the opening. The hands seemed to be pulling something out of the tree.

Sophie stood up and didn't budge. She thought about running, but she did not think her legs would obey her. She was breathing fast, and it felt like her heart was beating a million miles a minute. What was happening? What was coming out of the tree? Did it have to do with the head of the statue inside the tree?

Unexpectedly, a woman's head popped through the opening, and then her shoulders. Her body emerged more and more, and her legs stepped out. Sophie could see that she wore a beautiful gossamer dress in shades of lavender that swirled around her ankles as she stepped onto the ground.

Sophie wrapped her arms around herself and stared in wide-eyed astonishment. The woman stood up and turned to walk toward her. Sophie was frozen to the rock where she was standing. She felt afraid and happy, but she could not remember when she had ever felt both feelings so strongly in her body at the same time.

The woman had a warm smile on her face, and as she walked closer she seem to get taller. She shook her head to free her hair, and it seemed to grow instantly. Sophie noticed a golden crown of stars on her head. When she opened her arms and hands, it struck Sophia that the Golden Lady seemed to be saying, "Welcome to my home." It was clear to Sophie that it was an invitation.

Sophie could see through the magnificent Golden Lady to the trees behind her. It was not until she looked directly into her eyes that she saw love and goodness, and then Sophie relaxed. There was no room for fear. For several seconds, all that existed in the world were those angelic eyes.

The divine Golden Lady moved a little closer, and a scrumptious fragrance began to drift through the air. It reminded Sophie of the scent of roses. She did not just smell the fragrance; she felt it.

The Golden Lady spoke to her in a voice that sounded like singing bells and silver chimes. So sweet was the sound that Sophie felt tears in her eyes—just from hearing her voice.

"Sophie, thank you for awakening me. Your gentle touch has called me back onto the earth. It is good to be back. I see that my messenger has brought you."

The blue butterfly, as if realizing it was being addressed, fluttered low to the ground like it was bowing to her. She spoke again, "Thank you for coming, my dear girl. It is wonderful to meet you at last."

At the moment, Sophie was not sure she could even speak, so she sat in silent awe, taking in all that was unfolding in front of her. The Golden Lady swept past her, turned, and with her hand gestured to the tree as if she were introducing it to Sophie.

"This tree has been my home on earth for eons. It is called the Tree of Life, and it is the most beautiful tree ever created. Philosophers have written about it throughout the ages. The tree holds many secrets of your world. Do you like it?" she asked Sophie.

All Sophie could do was nod her head, and in a whisper say, "Yes, it's magnificent!"

"I agree," she said, smiling down at Sophie. "Do you know who I am?"

Sophie shook her head. "No, Golden Lady. I'm afraid I do not know who you are."

"I'm not surprised. Most every being in your world has forgotten. I'm the Goddess of Wisdom," she informed her.

When she said that, Sophie felt a shiver go down her spine, and she knew what she had heard was true.

"Once upon a time, all people knew of me and came for counsel. Wisdom was highly prized. You had only to whisper my name, and I was there. I have been called by many names and written about in all of the world's important books."

"My heart is full of compassion and I live in every human heart, although many have shut me out. I live in every part of nature and the universe. I am hope where there is darkness and ignorance. I have decided to return and restore my wisdom to the world, so that anyone can walk a path of beauty, truth, and wisdom."

She asked, "Do you know what my name is?" and looked directly into Sophie's eyes. "It's a name you are familiar with," and she gave a gentle little laugh.

The joyful sound of the goddess' laughter overwhelmed Sophie. Nothing could surpass the feeling that swept through her—not even receiving every Christmas present that she had been given in her whole life—all at once.

"My name is SOPHIA," the Golden Lady stated clearly.

"And your true name, my dear, is also Sophia."

Sophie stared in disbelief. They both shared the same name.

"Yes!" the goddess said, smiling fully. "We have the same name. You are also wise, young lady."

"That is why I have asked you to come, dear one. I have a monumental task that must be done if my wisdom is to come back into this world. I will need a brave girl to help me do this." She looked right at Sophie, who was still digesting what she had stated about their names being the same.

Goddess Sophia continued to speak. "Much has been lost of the true meaning of womanhood. There is much wisdom to be learned and shared. I believe that it is time for me and my sisters to return and bring wisdom back to women—and to girls just like you. I want to restore their belief in themselves, help renew their inner wisdom, and teach them to love every tiny part of their bodies—just as they are."

Before Sophie could ask her what she meant by her *sisters*, the goddess went on speaking. "The task I ask of you is to find the missing pieces of the statue for the courtyard at the Temple of the Seven Sisters—the one your grandparents are uncovering."

"The Oracle statue that you have been told about was of me, the Goddess Sophia. When my statue and all its pieces have been restored and the golden crown of stars placed on my head, I can awaken my sisters, who are represented by the statues standing behind me in the plaka of my temple."

"My sister goddesses will then be freed and brought to life. They will share their unique lessons of wisdom with young girls and women everywhere. My sister goddesses shall live again, as shall I."

"It is an important task, and one I do not ask lightly of you, Sophie. You have already found my statue's head that dwells in the tree. Now, you must find the arms of the statue, my torso, and my legs and place them all together on top of the pedestal. Once my body is whole again, and the golden crown of stars is placed on my head, you will see for yourself how wisdom shall once again be restored. Will you help me?" she asked.

Sophie was now staring down at the ground, feeling all of her own doubts and fears. She felt unworthy of the task. "Goddess Sophia, I'm not sure you want me to help you. I don't think you have the right girl. I'm not brave and I struggle with how I feel about myself, my body—just everything." Sophie looked up now at the goddess. "I don't see how I could do this for you, although I want to."

"My darling girl, it is because you struggle that I know you are perfect for the task. I do not seek perfection in you; I seek wisdom in you. Wisdom comes from overcoming what holds you back. Look beyond your limitations. This is an invitation to see truth where only doubt seems to exist."

The goddess gazed at Sophie with love. It was a love bigger than family, bigger than friends, bigger than any love she had ever felt before. In that moment surrounded in this love, Sophie felt a strength that was hard to put into words. It filled her from her toes to the top of her head. Who could deny such compassion and such love?

"Okay, I will find the rest of your statue, and I will help wisdom come back into the world. We need it," she said, with strength back in her voice. "How can I do this? I don't have any idea how to start."

Again the goddess spoke; her voice carried an air of lightness. "Use the intuitive skills you have begun to discover inside yourself. Let your open heart guide you in accomplishing this task. Remember, if you are to do this, you will have to overcome your own doubts, fears, and judgments of yourself and your body."

"I will send you help, but you must remember to ask for my wisdom. It may come in many forms—everything from my sisters' inspirations to the forces of nature itself. You must remember to look for wisdom in unexpected ways."

Sophie asked one more question, "Can Tena help me?"

The goddess nodded her head. "Yes, of course she can help you."

Abruptly, Sophie sensed an unseen force was gathering strength. It rolled across the green grass and up the tree. It seemed to expand and grow stronger. Sophie knew instinctively that it was the Goddess Sophia gathering the energy around her. Her light became bright, but Sophie could still clearly make out the details of her face, although she was invisible.

It seemed that the goddess had the wings of a butterfly. The goddess then looked at Sophie fully. "I have one last truth to tell you that will help you in performing this task. Remember this, for it will provide you the greatest strength you have ever known."

The goddess hesitated and she said with authority, "You, Sophie, are a *BORN GODDESS!*"

With that, she seemed to disappear, turning into a million little lights sparkling and spraying out in every direction. Sophie felt a mighty wind begin to blow. Goddess Sophia's last words echoed in her body streaming through Sophie's mind and heart. She was a *Born Goddess*—an inheritance she didn't completely understand, yet.

The wind blew stronger. Sophie lifted up so quickly that she had no time to think about what was happening to her. She was carried back across the forest, over the moonlit land, through her window, and plunked onto her bed.

Sophie felt goose bumps all over, and lit up from the inside out. This, without a doubt, was the most unbelievable dream she had ever had. Although she felt awake, she soon found herself slipping into a state of sleep.

In the morning, when she woke up—this time for real—she enthusiastically recorded every detail of her dream adventure in her journal. She did not want to forget a single detail.

Then she thought to herself, "Was that a dream, or did it really happen?" It seemed to Sophie that there was only one way to find out.

Chapter 12
Sophia's Face

Sophie jumped out of bed and put her journal in the nightstand drawer. She felt like she was on fire. She ran into the shower and got ready in record time. She bounded downstairs only to find Nina in a grumpy mood. It seemed the whole crew had cleaned out the refrigerator and left the kitchen a mess the night before.

Nina announced to no one in particular, "I have to go to the city to get more supplies." She slammed her purse around and finished writing a list of supplies she needed to buy. She said to Sophie, "I won't be back until late today. Can you take care of yourself this morning?"

"Yes, of course." Sophie replied.

Nikos was sitting outside in the van with the engine running, waiting to take an unhappy Nina to town. Sophie ran out and asked Nikos, "Can you let my grandparents know I have things to do this morning and will come to the site late afternoon."

Nikos seemed distracted as Nina got into the van, tossing her purse up on the dashboard and folding her arms across her chest. She was displeased and did not care who knew it.

Sophie tapped Nikos on the arm. "Please promise me you'll tell them. I don't want them to worry."

Finally, Nikos looked at her. "Okay, Sophie. I hear you. I go right by the site on the way to town. I'll stop and tell them. Don't worry."

He put the van in reverse and swung out onto the road. He was kicking up quite a lot of dust as he bumped and banged down the road. He was going faster than he usually did, and Sophie imagined he was going to get quite an earful about the dirty kitchen and the empty refrigerator.

"Yes!" Sophie thought. "Now, my grandparents won't know what I'm up to today." She ran into the house, packed herself a lunch, grabbed a bottle of water, and wrote a note saying she would be back in the afternoon in case no one got the message from Nikos. Then, she bolted out the door.

Before she left, she went out to the tool shed and found a large canvas bag. She threw it over her shoulder and headed for the woods.

Sophie hiked rapidly up the path, passed by the inviting stream, and found herself wishing Tena was here with her. Well, she guessed she would just have to do this by herself.

When she got to the area where Sophie thought the hidden path should be, she hesitated, not sure it was the right spot. She made a false start and got a mouth full of leaves—this was obviously not the right place.

She walked on a bit farther. "Ah, yes, this has to be it." Sophie tried again to force her way through. The brambles scraped her arms and she was repelled back, bleeding only slightly, but now she was mad.

Sophie stepped back and threw the canvas bag on the ground. Nina was not the only one who was having a bad day! She paced back and forth. "So, it *was* just a dream. *Born Goddess*, huh? What was that supposed to mean, anyway?

A few feet farther down the path, she tried to shove her way through the thicket, again. This time she got smacked by a tree branch. It hit her squarely in the face. "Ouch! That hurt!" Now, she was really irritated.

"Help!" she yelled. "Where is some help? Goddess Sophia told me she would give me her help, but nothing is working. Where is the help?"

Sophie walked across the path, sat down on the edge of the road, and felt like crying. But she talked herself out of it. After all, she was twelve years old and crying was not an option.

She finally closed her eyes and thought about the dream. She went over the details of what she had been told. Then it hit her. She wasn't using what Tena had shared with her—what Tena had learned from her mother. "Well, then start being wise," she said to herself. "Calm down, get connected, and find your open heart."

Sophie closed her eyes and placed her hand over her heart the way Tena had shown her. Her breathing began to slow down as her thoughts returned to the turtle. If she had tried to touch the turtle in the state she was in right now, she would have never been able to get close to him, let alone touch a wild creature. She was in a frustrated state, and that wasn't where she wanted to be.

So, she started over again, slowing her mind and breathing more calmly. "Think about love," she thought. Pictures of the people she loved came floating into her mind, and she took her time thinking and feeling into each person. She imagined Athena in the Parthenon and the nod she had given her.

Perhaps the Goddess Athena had been letting her know about this task that she was going to accept. She knew she was on the right track when the Goddess Sophia's face and the scent of roses came rushing into her mind.

She said softly, "Goddess Sophia, show me. Lend me your wisdom, please." She then felt the connection she had with the Goddess of Wisdom and she opened her eyes.

She got up, picked up the canvas bag, and stood there feeling the pull of wisdom—as if it were pulling her forward. It was strong in her body. Two pale yellow butterflies were fluttering along the edge of the path, so she followed them. They traveled back to the spot where she had first tried to go through the hedge. She checked to make sure no one was around. She saw one little butterfly slip into the hedge, and then the other followed. Okay! She followed them.

This time, Sophie did not push her way through the thicket. Instead, she just gently eased into the brush. She imagined that Tena was leading the way—first one foot, then another and another. Before she could even think about it, she was through to the other side.

"Wow! That was easy," she said aloud. "Easy, if you have an open heart." She looked around and the butterflies were gone. She was all alone in the woods. She noticed how the woods were darker, and without Tena she could have easily felt afraid. But it was not a false bravery that was moving her now. It was the feeling of wisdom. It was powerful, and it told her that she was safe and to keep going.

Sophie walked over the crumbled stones of the old road, down the winding path, and into the green forest. She went up the hill where the old remnants of the road ended. Once over the crest of the hill, the gigantic tree that belonged to Wisdom was finally visible and filled her vision in all directions. The dream came back to her, and she felt the hairs on the back of her neck perk up.

Sophie walked straight over to the tree. She set the bag on the ground, climbed up the roots and looked inside the opening. She had a flashlight this time, and she flashed it directly on the statue's face. Yes, she was still there.

Sophie stepped off the roots and sat down to look at the opening. She had several issues to contemplate. There was the problem of getting the statue's face out of the tree. It was most certainly wedged in there, and physically part of the tree by now.

She wondered how she would be able to carry it since it probably weighed about fifty pounds. Sophie was strong, but that would be a lot to handle walking all the way back to the house.

"Well, Goddess Sophia, how am I going to do this?" she asked out loud. She waited, but no booming voice answered her. What had she expected?

She began by walking around the tree, eyeing it deliberately as she went. As she rounded the outer corner she almost walked into a huge spider web that stretched in all directions. She found herself looking directly at a large black spider with yellow spots on its body.

Sophie had not really liked spiders most of her life and now one dangled just inches in front of her face. She realized she was holding her breath and she put one foot behind her moving slowly backwards. She let out a sigh of relief because she had just missed walking directly into the spider.

The spider's web went high up into the trees branches and

down onto the roots. Its threads stretched out in all directions, while other threads spiraled all the way from the center in tiny rows to the outside edges. Each thread connected to another so that all the threads supported each other. Just looking at it was a wonder, it was a true masterpiece. "Could any human being have woven a better web than this spider?" Sophie thought.

The spider sat contently close to the center of her web. Sophie thought that the spider's eight eyes were looking in different directions and, surely, several of those eyes were looking at her. Sophie stepped back to get a better view. It amazed her that all those hundreds and hundreds of threads had been created from just one spider's body.

Sophie sat down now less afraid. She knew she was supposed to be thinking about how she was going to get the face of Wisdom out of the tree, but she just had to keep looking at the spider. "What am I to learn from you?" she wondered.

Just then the wind blew and the web swayed and stretched out and back again. A tiny thread broke and the spider went over to investigate. It took her no time to repair it. Next, a leaf fell on the web and the spider turned slightly, but did not run to look at it. Sophie thought, "She knows it's a leaf, she didn't have to look at it, she just felt it."

Before long, a fly passed through the web, but circled back. It was caught and the spider quickly scurried across the threads to get the fly. She knew exactly what to do. Again, the spider had known it was a fly by the way it touched the web—her web tells her everything she needs to know because it's her Web of Life.

Still fascinated, Sophie took out her sandwich and water, and quietly ate while studying the spider. Shortly, Sophie began to feel her heart opening. She closed her eyes and thought of Wisdom looking at her in her dream. She could feel her body begin to change.

She opened her eyes, but the feeling of love remained. In fact, the more she thought about love, the more she felt her heart grow. She placed her hand on her heart, which seemed to make the feeling grow even stronger.

The spider knew what was going on in her world by the way things felt on her web. Sophie remembered what Tena had said about how everything was connected and not separate. She then realized that she had just had that kind of connection with the turtle, a creature of the wild, a few days before. Was it because she had opened her heart and filled it with love like Tena had suggested?

"Wow," Sophie thought, "what if I'm like the spider. What if my thoughts and feelings were like the threads of a web? What am I capable of knowing if I follow *those* threads?"

Just as each thread on the spider's web was connected to the other threads, each thought and feeling in Sophie's heart was connected to her next thought and feeling. It became clear to her that she could discover answers by following those threads.

"This is intuition," she thought. "It is not magic, but patience and paying attention to my feelings—and letting my heart guide me." This was the Web of Life, and watching the spider had taught her how to follow her intuition.

She leaned back and stretched out on the cool moss and grass. She kicked off her shoes and looked up into the giant arms of the tree. Somewhere in all that looking she closed her eyes, but did not sleep. She felt like she was feeling a place inside of her that she had never felt before. What was it the goddess had said? Something about overcoming her own fears? Yes! She had to overcome how she felt about her limitations and that included her feelings about her body, too.

Sophie imagined the threads of the Web of Life stretching inside her and imagined the face of the Goddess of Wisdom watching her. This was the goddess' face, but what about her own face? Most of the time she did not like it. In fact, she did not like seeing herself in the mirror, either. Her girlfriends always told her there was nothing wrong with her nose, or anything else, for that matter.

Maybe they were just being kind. Whenever Sophie looked at her face and nose, well, it made her feel yucky! "I hate my nose," she thought.

The minute she thought that, her heart began to hurt. Tension came back into her shoulders, and she suddenly felt afraid and vulnerable lying in the grass all by herself in that secluded place in the woods.

Sophie quickly opened her eyes, sat up, and looked around. No one was there. Everything was fine. Bugs were buzzing and birds were flying among the tree branches. Boy, how fast that connection to wisdom could disappear. The Web of Life was gone in a matter of seconds. What was obvious was that her negative feelings about her nose were keeping her from loving herself. And knowing that was going to keep her from finding a solution to getting the statue's head out of the tree.

Sophie shifted her thinking and her feelings back to having an open heart. That was the key. She immediately 'knew' she was safe again because she could *feel* it. She lay back and closed her eyes. She was like a spider, again sitting in the Web of Life, and she followed the first thread back to her feelings about her nose.

This time she did not flinch. She imagined how her nose looked and the shape of her face and added her hair this time, too. What was so wrong with them? So what if she didn't look like a movie star or a super model. Who did she look like, then?

She kept following the thread, and just like a spider's web, it connected and linked to another thread. Okay, so she had her grandmother's nose. Even her dad had said that. She followed another thread, and she was reminded of pictures she had scrap-booked of her grandmother and her great-grandmother. The old pictures burned bright in her mind and her heart. "These women are part of me, and part of my body and my life. When I complain about my nose and think I'm ugly, I'm calling all these wonderful women of my family ugly, too."

She had heard family stories about how each woman was special and did specials things to help others. And then there was her father, too, whom she loved very much. Was this all part of the web of *her* life? Her great-grandmother had made many sacrifices by coming to America to provide a better life for her children. It seemed empowering to belong to such a family.

The connection shifted to another thread of the web, and Sophie felt how much she truly loved these people for who they had been and who they were. "Am I," she wondered, "disrespecting them and not appreciating all of the other wonderful things about them?"

Another thread came forward. To be honest, even the statues of the goddess had the same Greek nose that she had. This thought led her back to the words of the Goddess Sophia. What else had she said? You are a *Born Goddess*? You have to open to the Goddess Wisdom inside of you.

Now, Sophie was beginning to get it. Inside she was made up of the wonderful people who were her family. If that meant her nose was different than the models in a magazine, so be it! Her

inheritance was much larger and far more powerful than she had been seeing. Like Métis' description of a caterpillar that only sees what is right in front of it, she had not seen the 'big picture.'

She had to be a butterfly and fly higher to see a larger view of herself. She needed to appreciate everything about herself. To be free to like herself was a wonderful gift.

Wow! Sophie had come full circle and proclaimed: "I love my nose and my face and my hair. I sincerely do!" She leapt to her feet and did a little victory dance right there in the middle of the secret forest. She felt fantastic.

Now, she knew what to do. She climbed up onto the roots of the tree and shined her flashlight inside. She wedged the flashlight gently into the edge of the tree opening so her hands would be free, then whispered, "Goddess Sophia, help me be wise."

She talked softly to the tree as if it were a living being, since it was. "This is what I want to do, great tree. I want to remove the head of the statue of Goddess Sophia and take it back to the temple site. Doing this will restore her glory so we can all benefit from her wisdom once again."

"Will you help me, will you release the face of the goddess?" she asked the tree.

Sophie waited—then opened her heart. She felt her connection to the tree and recognized that this was part of the Web of Life. She loved this tree; it was old and beautiful. From where she stood she could see the spider and the web, its threads connected to the tree limbs high above. Just looking at the spider helped give her courage to continue and trust her instincts. Confidently, she reached into the tree with one hand, and then the other. She balanced herself by leaning her arms more strongly against the outside of the tree, and it felt like the tree was holding her.

She moved her small fingers around each side of the face, which was now looking right at her. Gently, like touching the turtle's back, she began to pull, ever so carefully.

Was it her imagination or did the head move slightly? She took a deep breath and kept feeling the love she had felt in the goddess' eyes in last night's dream. She even felt a genuine feeling of love for her own face, her nose included.

Yes! It had moved. She felt it give. She kept pulling, gingerly. It

moved some more. It seemed like the opening of the tree was moving, too. All of the sudden, the head was suspended in her small hands. As if by some other force, she lifted it up easily, slowly moving it closer to being free of the sides of the tree.

In one breathless movement, it came free and she pulled the marble head from the opening. With it held gently in her hands, Sophie took another deep breath and cautiously walked down the roots of the tree and onto the grass.

She placed the goddess' face on the ground and quickly went to retrieve her flashlight. Then she returned, sat down, and picked the head up to look at in the full light. She thought of the goddess in her dream and how the sculptor most surely had seen her, too. Every nuance of the statue's face was the same as she had seen on Goddess Sophia's face in her dream.

Sophie could hardly believe that the statue's head was free from the tree. She was relieved that she had found a way to make it happen. She was also aware that she had not retrieved the statue's face all by herself.

So, she stood up in front of the tree, spread her arms out to her sides, and bowed. "Thank you for helping me free Wisdom."

She looked up at the sky and, thinking of Wisdom, said to herself, "Thank you for showing me a larger way to see my world."

Sophie tenderly wrapped the goddess' head in a towel she had brought with her and placed it in her canvas bag. She knew it was now late in the afternoon, but she was walking effortlessly as the marble sculpture seemed to weigh no more than a feather. She walked back down the hill, following the stone road. She quickly found the green wall and with Goddess Sophia's marble face cradled safely in her arm, she stepped easily through the hedge.

She peered down the path to make sure no one was coming. There was no one anywhere.

Sophie walked back with a freer spirit. She liked her own face. She was proud of her nose and her family heritage. For the first time in her young life, she could not wait to look in the mirror and celebrate what she saw.

She thought to herself, "A little wisdom is a wonderful thing."

Chapter 13

Demeter, Persephone, and the Secret of the Fire

This was no dream, she was actually holding in her hands the marble head of the statue of the Goddess Sophia. She could not take her eyes off the lovely carving.

No one had been home when Sophie arrived at the house, so she went straight to her room and shut the door. She was not quite sure what the professor or her grandparents would think about her having a piece of a statue in her room. Would they think of it as simply an artifact?

They were scientists, so how would the three of them react when they heard about her dream that now appeared to be real? She did not have an answer at the moment. What she felt she needed to do right now was protect the goddess' face, at least until she figured out what else she needed to do.

There was also the troubling question of all the other pieces of the statue she was to bring together. The thought of how she was supposed to do this overwhelmed her just thinking about it.

For now, she had protected the secret of the tree. No one knew where it was or how to find it. The fulfilling of the task had begun, and she had accomplished what, only the day before, she would have thought was impossible.

She turned the marble head from side to side, lovingly touching the brow and then the lips. Sophie was sad to leave the figure, but she wanted to see what was going on at the site.

Finding a safe place to keep the goddess' face was important and she decided on her traveling suitcase in the closet as the ideal place. No one would look there. She placed the marble head on a pillow and with loving care secured the suitcase so nothing would happen to the bag while it was in her closet.

Before she went any further, she walked into the bathroom adjacent to her bedroom. She turned on the light and stood squarely in front of the mirror. She had done this before, but it had not produced pleasant results. Sophie tested out her new feelings by looking at herself in the mirror. Her hair was loose and curly, but it looked healthy and shiny—something she had not noticed before.

Her face and its shape looked just fine. Her eyes were lovely and expressive, and she could not believe that she had never noticed them before.

She had saved her nose for last. She leaned in and examined it thoroughly. She looked at it from one side, and then from the other. She wrinkled it and stretched it and let it just be itself on her face. She had to admit that it looked perfectly normal. It fit her face and made her look strong, even clever. Her conclusion was that it was a good nose, even a handsome nose.

So, what had been the big deal? She looked deeply into her eyes and announced, "Sophie, you truly *are* a Born Goddess!" She could not help but give a little giggle. It felt so comfortable to look at herself— and like what she saw.

Before Sophie headed out, she grabbed a package of snack crackers and a granola bar. Over the stony landscape she hustled, heading straight for the site and the crew.

It was about three o'clock in the afternoon, which was usually close to the end of the day for the camp. However, spirits were high and there seemed to be a feeling of urgency in the air when she arrived. Was it that Sophia and her sisters were urging everyone on? Whatever it was, the site was abuzz with excitement.

Sophie's grandparents quickly spotted her, and of course her grandfather gave her a chocolate bar. He had set up a chair for her, just like before. She got out her camera, all charged and ready to take pictures.

Diane was standing on a ladder with a trowel and brushes tucked in her belt. Large amounts of dirt had been removed from between the two statues. In the course of removing the soil, they had found two arms, each coming from different statues that met in the middle with one statue's hand holding the other statue's hand. It looked rather odd, since the statues remained totally immersed in dirt with only their arms exposed.

The professor was light on his feet today, dancing back and forth, keeping two teams working on the two statues. Diane was on the right with her team, and another graduate student named Beverley was on the left. Beverley had become friends with Sophie as they had found more chances to talk. She was tall and had brown hair with shiny golden tones. Right now she had her hair bundled under a red bandana, no doubt to keep the dirt out.

The professor was hustling about, shouting last-minute instructions. That was why he failed to see a rock lying close to the second statue. Diane was balancing on her ladder next to the statue using a small trowel. Abruptly, the professor rushed forward with a larger tool, a spade, announcing that Diane was going to need this one instead of the smaller trowel she was using.

He had no more than gotten the words out of his mouth when he stumbled. He went flying forward, tripping over the stone, and his large spade dug right into the dirt encasing the statue. When he fell forward, he bumped into Diane's ladder and she began to fall.

Diane grabbed onto the earthen shell around the statue, only to have her trowel, and her hands, dig deep into the dirt. As Diane and the professor were trying to right themselves, other team workers came rushing toward them to see if they were okay.

Stefan then bumped the second ladder with Beverley on it, and she let out a yell. She fell right into her statue smacking her face; for there was no place else to go. As she struggled she pushed hard against the earth around the statue to keep herself and her ladder from falling sideways.

Professor Conrad pulled his spade out and a large chunk of dirt went flying. When Diane pulled hers back, more dirt started falling. Amidst a crazy mangle of arms and legs, and people running right and left, the earthen shell around the statue cracked off in a large sheet, crashing against more earth on the statue's front as it fell. This created the effect of a mini avalanche, as sand and earth cascaded down to the ground.

Next, the earth on the other statue began sliding as Beverley scrambled to get out of the way. Sophie sat on the edge of her seat watching this calamity of errors, as earth peeled off the second statue. It plummeted downward pulling off more and more dirt as it fell, hitting the ground in large chunks. The workers, who were on their knees working behind the statue, had to jump to get out of the way. Everyone just stood in silence, helplessly watching it happen.

In a matter of minutes, the two statues were standing free, stripped of all debris. Everyone's mouth was hanging open. Someone finally yelled, "What just happened? Is everyone okay?"

What was supposed to have taken hours of probing and brushing had been accomplished in minutes. The professor, having pretty much recovered, was inspecting things closely to see if anything had been damaged. Sophie's grandparents were examining each of the statues—front and back. Yes, the arms were fine, the face, the nose, and the ears, even the hands were okay. Somehow both statues had escaped any damage, in spite of what just had happened.

Everyone began laughing. Tensions were released with hoots and yells. "Wow!" "Did you see that?" "Was that cool or what?" They were all talking at once. The workers were called in to help pile the soil and sand in wheelbarrows. The men shook their heads and chuckled as they bent to shovel the sand and earth off the ground.

Diane, having recovered from nearly crashing to the ground, was cautiously brushing damp sand from the crevices of eyes and mouth of the statue. Soon, everyone had a brush and was working furiously to clean the surfaces of both statues. An hour later, when they had cleared away all the loose dirt and sand, two beautiful new statues stood majestically overlooking the area.

Sophie's grandmother came over and explained that the first

statue was Demeter, the goddess associated with motherly love, kindness, and generosity. "She is one of the most famous mothers of mythology," she told her.

Demeter held a bundle of wheat in the crook of her arm, leaving her other arm and hand free to welcome the viewer. Her hair was full and she wore a cape that draped off one of her shoulders. Her eyes met those of the other figure with whom she was holding hands. The other goddess was her daughter, who her grandmother said was named Persephone. The two of them shared a powerful bond of mother-daughter love.

Sophie, once again, was in awe at the artistry of the sculptor. The artist had placed the two statues in the exact position so that their gaze never left each other's eyes. It sent a little shiver down Sophie's back because it felt so surreal to her.

By now the crew had recovered from the shock and surprise of what had happened. Professor Conrad was getting into the chaotic feeling of it all. It had been like an old-fashioned silent film where actors run into each other and narrowly miss clobbering one another. Everyone had moved into a high-spirited sense of fun once they realized that although everything had seemed to be falling apart, it had come together quite nicely.

The professor proposed that everybody follow him to town to celebrate. Sophie's grandparents looked tired and they declined. They said that they were going to walk back to the Blue House with Sophie and would meet at the site in the morning.

The craziness of the day had now started to catch up with Sophie, too, and she felt tired. Was it only this morning that she had retrieved the statue of Wisdom's face?

The three walked back across the hills talking about how this had been the fastest excavation work they had ever been involved in. Her grandfather quipped, "All I can say is that those two goddesses must have wanted to be freed tonight."

Sophie thought to herself, "Oh, Pa Pou, if you only knew."

It was getting chilly, since the sun was about to set. When they reached the house, Nina had built a fire in a side room that was like a den. She had laid out cold plates of thinly sliced meats and cheeses, with a fresh fruit plate in the refrigerator. There was a note on the counter with the receipts for the food she had purchased. Her note said she would be back in the morning to bake bread.

Sophie's grandparents talked about how bad they felt about ruining Nina's day. They promised they would make it up to her. It was not long before they headed off to bed, but Sophie stayed up to enjoy the fire a little longer.

This room with the fireplace was a comfortable, cozy room. It had a huge overstuffed couch and two big chairs. Books in many different languages lined the shelves because people often contributed them when they left to go back home.

Sophie finished eating her grapes and sat with her legs up on the couch watching the fire. The only fireplaces Sophie was familiar with were automatic ones in her friends' homes. This fire had been built with real wood. It snapped and crackled and smelled good. Its warmth was most welcome.

As Sophie relaxed she started thinking about her day. When she had first seen the clay discs that the professor had shown her, she had been intrigued with them. She had felt they were part of a puzzle and had even voiced the thought that the placement of the discs reminded her of a garden of seeds and flowers. She had asked Diane, who had made drawings of all the discs, if she would make copies of the drawings for her.

Just before she left the site this evening, Diane had handed Sophie a large plain envelope with copies of the drawings. Diane had leaned over and whispered in her ear, so no one else could hear, "We found more designs after you first saw them. Good luck with these pictures, and let me know what you figure out." She then gave Sophie a friendly wink.

Now, alone by the fire, Sophie pulled the drawings out of the envelope. The first one was of the owl, but Diane had added a shield behind it. Sophie had not seen the shield before, but because Diane meticulously cleaned all the artifacts before she made her drawings, Sophie knew it was definitely imbedded in the clay. That particular disc represented Athena and she recorded it in her journal.

She pulled out a drawing of a crescent moon and a bow and arrow. This disc symbolized the second statue they had found, which depicted Artemis.

Now, Sophie looked for a drawing of a disc that would represent

Demeter, Persephone, and the Secret of the Fire

Demeter. She found it—a bundle of wheat that matched today's statue. Sophie knew, because of her dream, that the Goddess Sophia had called all the statues her sisters. That had to mean that all the statues were goddesses. With this information she reasoned that each disc illustrated a statue and, therefore, was a goddess.

The next drawing showed a fruit, and she had to look at it closer to see if she could figure out what kind of fruit it was. Finally, she looked through Diane's notes, where she found a notation that identified it as a pomegranate. Sophie had read the myths of the Greek goddesses, and she tried to remember if any of them were connected to a pomegranate. Then, she remembered Persephone. That was it. She realized this disc most likely was associated with the daughter statue that had been so unexpectedly uncovered this afternoon.

Sophie turned to the next drawing. This one showed a fire burning in a circular dish. She laid the papers down and tried to remember everything about a goddess and fire. Earlier she had turned off the other lights in the room so she could enjoy just the light of the fire in the fireplace. She had been looking at the drawings by firelight, but now her eyes were getting heavy. She was not asleep, but she was not awake either. She was thinking, "Who are you, Goddess of the Fire?"

At that moment she heard a loud snap from the fireplace. She looked over and the fire seemed to be energized. She thought, "Who are you?" But this time she directed her thoughts to the fire itself as the fire grew brighter.

It was not hard to imagine that the flames were like a woman's hair. They flickered and flashed like hair caught in the wind. The way the wood was burnt in places she could also see a pair of black eyes looking at her. If she squinted a little, she could make out a whole face.

It was in this twilight place between sleep and wakefulness that she thought she heard a hissing sound from the wood and flames. "Hessstia," it whispered.

"What?" she thought, but did not move, since she was so comfortable.

"Hessstia," the sound came again. "I'm Hestia, the Goddess of Transcendence and Centeredness. I'm here to tell you to go find the BEEEEES."

Sophie stirred and opened her eyes wider to look more closely at the fire and to look around the room as well. No one was there besides her. Then, the fire seemed to have expended its energy and mysteriously began burning much lower, like it would soon go out. She faintly heard the sound one more time. "Hestia!" Then, the fire quietly went out.

Sophie managed to write this name and about the bees in her journal before she rolled over, pulled a quilt on top of her, and fell asleep right there on the couch.

Chapter 14

Focus

Tena arrived at the Blue House and found Sophie anxiously waiting for her. Sophie grabbed Tena's hand, took her upstairs, and shut the bedroom door behind them.

Tena loved Sophie's room and thought the mural on the wall was cool. But Sophie was pacing back and forth anxiously. "I had the most incredible dream," she began. "You will not believe it."

"Well, tell me," Tena pleaded. "I can't wait to hear it."

Sophie began with the story about her blue butterfly tapestry on the wall. She talked about the moon in her window and tried to act out everything—everything from flying out her bedroom window to standing in front of the tree. Tena listened intently, her expressions changing as Sophie described the Goddess of Wisdom and how she looked and what she said. By this time, Tena was perched on the edge of the bed, eagerly asking questions as Sophie spoke. She was now as excited as Sophie.

Then Sophie said, "I'm not finished yet. I have to tell you about what happened yesterday." For the first time, the thought occurred to Sophie that Tena might be angry because she had not waited until she could go with her. But Sophie hesitated only a moment before she continued. She felt she had to prove to herself that her dream was real, and that the Goddess of Wisdom was authentic.

Sophie twisted and fluttered her hands as she told Tena how she had tried unsuccessfully to get through the thicket. She described what had happened so Tena could laugh at the image of her being repeatedly smacked in the face by the bushes and the tree branch and clawed by the brambles. Sophie knew she was talking faster and faster, but Tena seemed to have no problem following her story. She continued by saying that once she got to the tree she knew she had to face her own fears. She also had to deal with her thoughts and feelings about her own face. When she finally finished, she breathlessly blurted out, "Are you angry that I did all this without you?"

Tena flopped back on the bed and exclaimed, "Of course not!" She seemed overwhelmed with all that she had heard—all the while trying to understand how so much could possibly have happened in just one day.

"Look," Tena added, "the Goddess of Wisdom said this task was given to you. It is your name that is the same as the Goddess Sophia's. I feel you did exactly what I would have done if the dream had been mine. I do have a question, though, that I'm dying to ask. Tell me where the goddess' face is. I want to see it for myself."

Sophie went to the closet and in a minute was putting the face of the Goddess of Wisdom in Tena's lap. Tena stared at the face for a long time. She seemed to be in a state of awe as she lovingly traced the goddess' face with her fingers.

Sophie kept quiet and just let her hold it for as long as she liked. "I have looked upon this face through the opening of the tree for a long time," Tena confessed. "I wondered if ever it might be free. Now, the spirit of Wisdom is going to come back into the world. This is an important day." She sighed a sigh of sweet joy.

"You have a task to perform, and I will help you all I can. But it is you who has been asked to do this meaningful mission," Tena said. "You will need to let your intuition lead you and your heart guide you. Now—we have work to do!" She gently slapped her legs. "Let's get started!"

The two of them put the marble head back into the closet. Sophie finished collecting the things she thought she might need and put them in her backpack. She was relieved that Tena was happy, rather than felt left out about what had happened. "Let's go to the site first. I want to show you what we've found so far."

They both went downstairs. When Nina saw the girls, she called them over, "I have lunch for you two." Sophie hugged Nina and told her how important she was to her.

"I want you to come to the site and see what's going on," she urged. Nina waved her hand and replied, "Your grandparents already asked me this morning. I'm going to bring my husband. He loves all the old stories, so we will come together." Nina seemed her old self again, as if a storm had passed.

The girls left the house, and Tena was still in high spirits from having seen the face. On the walk down to the excavation site, Sophie told her about how the two statues had accidentally been cleared of debris. She acted out the whole thing for Tena and they both were still giggling when they arrived at the site.

Everyone was moving slowly today, and Sophie felt it was probably because they had all stayed up late celebrating. She took Tena around to the statues and, having a bit of fun, said, "Now, Tena I would like to introduce you to your namesake, Athena." Tena, playing along, took a little bow.

Sophie moved on. "This is Artemis." She could tell that Tena was impressed by the beauty of each figure.

"And I want you to meet Demeter, the Great Mother, and her daughter, Persephone."

Tena had now slowed down and had an expression on her face that showed her amazement. She turned to Sophie. "I cannot remember ever seeing artwork this beautiful. It is as if they are all alive, yet made of stone."

Just then Beverley and Diane walked over and Sophie introduced them to Tena. "Did you know that Tena is short for Athena?" Diane asked. "That is one powerful name to have been given, young lady."

Beverley interjected, "Well, what about Sophie? Her name is a shortened form of Sophia. Do you both know that you have been given the names of goddesses that stand for wisdom?"

"Yes, we know," both girls said at once and giggled.

They walked over to the empty pedestal where the missing statue had once stood. "I would like to find this missing statue," Diane said. "Without it, I feel the temple is incomplete." They all agreed.

Diane went on, "Did I tell you that we think there are three more statues and probably two more columns on the other side?

"I didn't know that," Sophie admitted.

"I can't wait to see who they will be. Do you have any guesses?" Diane asked, turning to look at both girls. She had such a wonderful way of making her dark chestnut ponytail bounce when she talked.

Sophie spoke up. "Well, I'd like to know more about Hestia. Could one of you tell me about her?"

"Well," Beverley began, "she was associated with fire. Every house and public temple had a fireplace or hearth that was considered to be her home, and the fire, her body.

"I also think of her as the Goddess of Transcendence and Centeredness," Diane said. "When you sit quietly and look into the fire you have the opportunity to go inside and find wisdom. It is there that you hear your inner voice—the voice that has many answers."

Sophie felt a little chill run down her spine. She would not have remembered what had happened with the fire the night before if she had not made a drawing of it and written Hestia's name down. Now, Diane was saying exactly the same words Sophie thought she had heard the night before from the fire itself.

Tena asked, "Do you think Hestia will be next?"

Sophie replied, "Well, why not. I think she could be the next one." The two grad students looked at each other with mischief in their eyes.

"Let's bet on it," Diane suggested.

"Yea," said Beverley. "If you lose, you have to eat olives."

They all laughed at Sophie, who was wrinkling her nose. "Oh, no!" she groaned.

"No, not really," Beverley gave in. She gestured to Diane and continued. "We'll settle for two loaves of Nina's fabulous bread. And if we lose, you get our chocolate stash."

"Okay! You're on!" Sophie agreed playfully. They all did a high-five and parted company.

Focus

Diane looked over her shoulder and shouted, "I can almost taste that bread now." Her ponytail bounced in agreement.

Walking along beside Tena, Sophie said, "I think we should look for the missing pieces of the statue. Do you have any ideas about where to go?"

"Well, I don't know about the statue, but I would like to show you something that is not far from here," Tena proposed.

"Let's go!" Sophie said eagerly.

Tena led the way as they walked over rocky hills, leaving the site below them as they began to climb gradually up the hill behind the excavation area. They climbed over large flat grey rocks and came up over a ridge that opened onto a plateau.

The view was incredible. The whole area was filled with red and orange and yellow poppies. Shoots of wheat grew among the flowers, suggesting the plateau area had once been a field. The golden wheat created a multitude of colors with the play of light as it moved across the field.

The girls walked among the gently blowing flowers. Bowing slightly, Sophie turned to Tena. "I think we need crowns, don't you, Miss Wise One?"

Quickly catching on and holding the side of her blue jeans like a skirt, Tena curtsied and replied, "Oh, yes, my dear Wise One, we do need crowns."

They grinned at each other and began to pick the flowers and spires of wheat, gathering them in their shirttails so they could carry more.

The meadow was rich with bees flying about to collect nectar, and to her amazement Sophie saw tiny brightly colored humming birds darting among the red flowers. It was magical as they walked. There, in the middle of the plateau, Sophie saw some broken columns and knew that a temple must have stood on this spot long ago. They walked over to the ruins and sat down on the circles of broken columns. They spread out their harvest of poppies and wheat, and began to weave their flower crowns.

By the time they finished, they were hungry. Sophie got out the goodies Nina had fixed for them. They put on their crowns and ate in silence as they enjoyed the beauty of the place.

Finally, when Tena had finished eating, she said, "I think that Demeter and Persephone would have loved this meadow."

"So tell me their story," Sophie encouraged her.

"It is a long story and we need to be searching for the Goddess of Wisdom's statue."

"Well, tell me something about them anyway."

Tena explained that Demeter was the great Mother Goddess and protector of growing things, like the fields and orchards. Her gift was to make things grow stronger through generosity and nurturing. One day her daughter, Persephone, whom she loved, was taken from her in secret by the God of the Underworld, Hades. He wanted Persephone to be his wife."

"Demeter searched for Persephone and as she searched, she became weaker and weaker. During the time of Demeter's grief, all the fields and orchards died. The people were starving so they went to Zeus, Persephone's father, and asked him to intervene."

"Zeus made a deal with his brother Hades to return Persephone to her mother; however, in the underworld if you had eaten anything, you were destined to be there forever. Unfortunately, Hades had tricked Persephone into eating six seeds from a pomegranate, which meant she would have to be part of his world six months of every year."

"Demeter and her daughter were then able to be together in the spring and summer while, during the fall and winter, Persephone would be the Queen of the Underworld."

"That's quite a story," Sophie said. She closed her eyes and added, "You know, you're right. Demeter and her daughter would love this place. I can almost see them here in my imagination."

Sophie sat quietly. Then she spoke again. "Since I don't know where to search next, don't you think I need to ask her to help me?"

"Yes, I do," Tena agreed.

Sophie got up and looked around. She found a flat piece of stone that must have been a floor and they both stretched out. Thankfully, the shade of a tree protected them from the hot sun.

After a short time, Sophie began to open her heart and felt her connection to nature and wisdom growing stronger. She thought about the statues of Demeter and Persephone and how they were holding hands. Sophie loved her mother that way, too.

Focus

As she followed her thoughts and feelings, she soon realized she was thinking about her body. Just how did she feel about her body? She thought about how it was changing. She was not a little girl anymore and she was not a woman yet, either. She was right in between, and it sometimes felt awkward and even uncomfortable. "I'm like that caterpillar right now, as are all my friends back home, and even Tena, too."

It was that butterfly-self she returned to in her thoughts as she followed the Web of Life inside her mind. She had stressful days and awkward times, but it would be worth it. Changes in her body would result in new experiences and new ways of looking at the world. She began to appreciate her body just thinking about who she was now and who she might become.

She followed the threads of the web and to her amazement; she found there was a feeling deep inside of her about how she loved being a girl. Wisdom was ready to guide all girls, including her, to find a better way to live life. Demeter would say, "Nurture your body." Persephone would say "Listen to your intuition, follow your dreams."

At this moment, Sophie felt the ground rumble and shake. She would have been frightened except that she felt this was connected to her request for help. She remained in her heart and after a minute or so, the ground stopped rumbling.

She quickly sat up, as did Tena. They looked at each other, and Sophie said, "Did you hear and feel that?"

"Oh, yea!" Tena said. "I sure did."

They got to their feet. "Where did that rumbling come from?" Tena asked.

Sophie ran over to where the noise seemed to have been the loudest. In back of the small ruined temple, a wide ditch had opened up. The earth appeared to have split open, and they could see part of a statue's torso sticking out. Sophie could hardly believe her eyes. The girls grabbed each other's arms and jumped up and down, yelling with glee as they looked at the treasure lying exposed in the earth.

Both girls scrambled down and took a long look at the piece. Sophie looked at the bottom and she could see chisel marks where someone had separated it from the legs.

"We need to clean it, and then you know what I think?" Sophie asked excitedly.

"What? Tell me," said Tena.

"I think we need to take it to the site," Sophie suggested. "No one would understand where it came from. And without its base and feet, no one will even suspect it is part of the missing statue."

"You're right," Tena admitted. "So, how do we do it?"

"Well," Sophie went on, "let's get some tools and clean her, and then wrap her in a canvas tarp. Behind the site there are a lot of tarps, and many of them are wrapped around pieces of equipment. No one has unwrapped or moved any of those things since we arrived at the dig. We will hide the statue right in plain sight. Afterwards, when we've found all the other pieces, we'll have to figure out how we're going to put them together."

"Whoa! When I asked, 'How do we do it?' I meant, how are we going to *move* it?" Tena said. "It's got to weigh a ton."

"You know, I thought that about the marble head, but I carried it easily. I think Wisdom helped me. Maybe she'll help me again."

"Well, before we do anything, let's try it and see."

So, the girls split up, one at the shoulders, the other at the lower part of the statue. When they grabbed each end and lifted up, the statue came loose from the earth easily. Tena looked shocked, but Sophie was confident. They walked it over to the side, where it was grassy. Okay, moving the statue was obviously not going to be a problem. So, they decided Sophie would go to the campsite and get what they needed, and Tena would stay and guard the torso.

It did not take Sophie long at the site, because she knew where everything was kept. She slipped in and out without anyone seeing her. When she came back up into the meadow, Tena looked relieved. Sophie showed Tena how to use the brushes, and they cleaned the torso of the Goddess Sophia. They laid out the canvas, set her in it, secured it, and began to move her.

Walking slowly, but steadily, they crossed the meadow and were ready to walk around to the back side of the site. Everything had gone well until Sophie started thinking about how heavy the statue should be. Her mind took over and suddenly her end of the statue dropped straight to the ground. Sophie barely had time to get her fingers out of the way.

"What's wrong?" Tena cried out as she let her end drop, too. She found that she could not hold her end up, once Sophie let go.

"It got so incredibly heavy, I *had* to drop it." Sophie confessed.

"Why?" Tena asked, suddenly out of breath. "Why now and not earlier? What happened?"

"I don't know. Really I don't," Sophie responded.

"Well," said Tena, "*something* happened."

Sophie just stood there. "Well, I did begin to think about how much this torso must weigh. I started thinking that we should not be able to do this at all."

Tena walked toward Sophie, and quietly said, "Remember the turtle and removing Wisdom's face from the tree?"

"When you put the power of your thoughts on one idea—that is called focus. Focus will create the result you want."

"The power of your doubts made the statue heavy again, so you could not carry it. When you stopped believing you could lift the statue, you dropped it."

Tena looked straight into Sophie's eyes, "Where you place the focus of your mind makes all the difference in the world as to how things will go in life. She spoke strongly, but lovingly. "Please open your heart and remember what you have already done. You can do this, *we* can do this."

Sophie nodded her head and waited as she cleared her mind of her feelings of doubt. She pulled the power of her thoughts back to the place where she believed she could lift the statue. It took a bit of time, but Tena was patient and waited quietly.

Sophie recognized the feeling as the warmth of her open heart came back. "Focus!" she thought to herself. She reached down and the statue came right up into their hands.

They carried it the rest of the way to the hill behind the site and waited in the trees to make sure there was no movement down below. They walked it down to the other canvas bundles and placed their treasure on the ground among the other things. It looked right at home. How perfect. No one was going to know it was there until the two of them revealed it.

They joyfully patted one another on the back and decided to call it a day. Before they left, Sophie whispered to the earth, "Thank you, Demeter and Persephone. Without your help, we would not have found Wisdom's body today."

Chapter 15
Little Details, Big Ideas!

Sophie came into the den and stood next to the large wooden library table. The morning sun was bright coming through the windows. She waited until she had her grandparents' attention, since they were both working on their laptop computers rather intently. Shortly, her grandfather looked up and asked, "What can we do for you, kiddo?"

Sophie laid her papers on the table. "I'd like to explain a theory I'm working on." In archaeology, the word *theory* is a way of presenting your thoughts on a subject to the people you work with. She knew this would show she was serious about what she wanted to tell them.

"Well, pull up a chair, and let's hear it," her grandfather said. Her grandmother saved her document and then they both looked at her. She felt a little embarrassed.

"It's about the clay discs. Remember?"

"Oh, yes," her grandmother nodded. "Your garden idea," she added, and shot an amused look at Sophie's grandfather. Sophie did not hesitate. She laid out her copies of Diane's drawings and got her own notes and spread them on the big table. She had sketched a drawing that showed the placement of the clay discs.

Sophie pulled up her chair, so she could lean in closely, and began. She went through each disc and its symbol. She showed how she thought each symbol corresponded to a goddess statue. She chose the shield with the owl and connected it to Athena, then the bow and arrow that related to Artemis. The wheat bundle was clearly Demeter, and the pomegranate was Persephone.

"Now," she continued, "there are three discs remaining and three statues to be identified." She looked back and forth at her grandparents to make sure they were following her.

She pulled forward Diane's drawing. "This picture shows fire on an alter. Fire is associated with the Goddess Hestia. The next is a scalloped seashell, and I feel it represents Aphrodite, the Goddess of the Sea."

"The third one is a bird, and not just any bird, it is a peacock. I was really stuck on that one," she said. "So, I went to the computer and did a web search. I typed in *peacock* and *goddess* and do you know how many sites I got?"

"No!" her grandfather responded with a surprised look on his face.

"It had over one million nine hundred thirty thousand sites and luckily I found exactly what I was looking for. Do you want to know what the goddess' name is?"

Her grandfather merely nodded his head.

"It's the Goddess Hera and I read that she teaches the virtues of friendship to young women."

"So, I think these are the identities of the statues you are going to discover in the next few days." Sophie sat with her hands on the drawings and waited to see their reactions.

"Well, that's good, Sophie," her grandmother said in a serious tone.

Her grandfather interjected, "Sophie, we've been so busy unearthing the statues and making measurements and doing calculations, I just haven't paid much attention to those clay discs. They seemed a minor detail in view of what we were finding. I never looked at them the way you have."

Sophie's grandmother continued, "If you are correct, we could have known the statues' identities earlier if someone had taken the time to think this through. It goes to show that even the smallest detail can have the biggest meaning."

She reached out and patted Sophie's shoulder. Her whole feeling had changed from amusement to support. "That was good scientific reasoning," she added. "I think you may have cracked the puzzle wide open. Don't you think so, George?" George had a huge grin on his face and looked like he was on fire with ideas.

Sophie leaned forward again. "I've one more idea, too!"

"Okay," said her grandfather. "Go for it."

"Well, Diane told me that a new disc was found just last week, and I feel that it completes the picture of the temple's meaning."

"So, what is it?" her grandmother asked.

"It's a disc with a crown of stars. I did research on the Internet for possible answers; the one I feel is right is associated with the Goddess of Wisdom. If I'm correct," Sophie continued, "that could mean the identity of the missing statue is Goddess Sophia."

Her grandparents began debating back and forth. "No, maybe it wasn't Sophia, but some other goddess." "Well, perhaps it was her."

And on they went, discussing the pros and cons of Sophie's idea. When they finally stopped, they admitted, "Well, Sophie you could be right about this."

Sophie was thinking of what to do. She was still positive that she shouldn't tell them about her dream, or the fact that she knew her analogy was correct because she had already found parts of the missing statue. She longed to tell them, but something deep inside of her kept saying, "Wait. Not yet, just wait."

"I want to show you how I think it works," she continued. She pulled out her large drawing of all the discs as they had been grouped together. "The discs with the crown of stars formed a row all around the others, like a fence," she explained. "It seemed to bind them all together. The other discs formed neat rows inside this Goddess Sophia frame. The rows were of a flower set, then another goddess set, then a flower set and a goddess set, and so on." She pointed to the drawing. "Remember my idea about this being a garden?'"

Her grandparents nodded their agreement. Yes, they remembered.

"I started thinking that maybe it depicted a field, not a garden."

She could see that her grandmother was following right along with her as she spoke.

Then her grandmother said, "All of these goddesses are connected with nature in some way. If this temple was intentionally buried, the Ancients were giving us a clue—one they thought would be obvious to us."

Now her grandfather chimed in, and she noticed he had reached out and was holding her grandmother's hand. "Sophie, you thought the symbolic discs of the goddesses were seeds. Perhaps this was the Ancients' way of saying they were giving us a field of ideas, food for our minds to harvest in our own time. Oh, my," he added, "the possibilities are endless."

"I would like to say one more thing," Sophie interrupted. "What I have learned, since I have been here in Greece, is that perhaps the Ancients were planting food for our hearts, not just our minds. They could be saying, too, that they are growing goddesses for us to harvest."

"I like that, sweetheart," her grandmother smiled. "This is impressive. I'd like to tell the professor about it."

"Yes, please," Sophie, said. "Let's see if I'm right."

"We'll know whether or not the first part of your theory is correct as soon as we unearth the remaining statues," her grandmother reminded her.

Her grandfather was now way ahead of them. "I think we should write a paper on this, and I'm going to give Sophie credit for it."

Her grandmother looked at her proudly. "Sophie, this is a sophisticated set of ideas. How did you come to it?"

Sophie sat back and smiled. "Oh, it's just intuition. That's how I figured it out."

The idea of knowing the identity of the future statues was so exciting that her grandfather jumped to his feet and announced, "This calls for a slice of Nina's bread and some honey to celebrate." He went charging into the kitchen. Her grandmother shook her head smiling, and all she said was, "Food!" and they both laughed.

Later that day, when the next statue was being unearthed, her grandparents and the professor were not surprised to find that Sophie had been correct. Yet it was hard to believe a twelve-year-old girl had seen what they hadn't.

Hestia was standing next to a long rectangular alter that had a metal bowl with fire burning it it. The flames looked like golden-colored quartz crystal. Her face showed warmth and there was an inviting feeling about her.

Diane leaned over and said quietly to Beverley, "There goes our chocolate stash." Smiling, she added, "I guess we lost the bet."

Earlier Sophie's grandparents had taken the time to explain to the professor the ideas she had put together about the discs. He was shocked that Sophie was right. He commented that she should be here to see all they were finding. Unfortunately, no one knew where Sophie was—just that she was exploring with Tena, somewhere in the woods.

Chapter 16
The Bees of Artemis

Sophie and Tena had been walking for over an hour going deeper and deeper into a remote part of the forest.

As they walked Sophie told Tena what had happened to her the other night. "After everyone had gone to bed, I sat on the couch and stared into the fire. In fact, I almost fell asleep. Maybe I was asleep when I heard a voice say, 'I'm Hestia.'"

"I knew that it came from the fire. Then I heard Hestia speak again, ever so softly, like a hiss of smoke. "'Find the BEEEEEES!' Just like that, and then the fire went out."

After hearing this part of the story, Tena stopped and told Sophie she thought she knew what Hestia had meant about the bees. "I know a place in the forest where the largest hive of bees I have ever seen is located. I've only been to this place once because I found it by accident. I think I can find it again, but it could be dangerous. When I was there, I did see a white rock close to the hive. Maybe it's part of the statue. But...bees can be unpredictable and dangerous."

Chapter 16

"Well, I may be crazy, but I feel we must go," Sophie said.

Sophie knew it had to be the place Hestia was talking about. So, off they went in search of the beehive. Once they left the safety of the path, Tena told Sophie that they should listen for the drone of the bees as it would guide them to the hive.

"How many bees does it take to make a sound you can hear that far away from the hive," she had wondered. The closer they got to the hive, the louder the sound. It had started as a quiet 'hmmmmm' and then got louder and louder. Now, it was so loud you could not hear anything over the sound of the bees.

There it was. The hive was several yards wide and cascaded over a tree trunk. It was like nothing Sophie had ever seen before. She thought of the pictures of nice little hives in storybooks and cartoons. She had even gone to a farm with her school class and they had built little houses for the bees to live and work in. But this was much different—this was powerful and wild and totally the bees' creation.

The hive was filled with thousands of bees. It was their home. They protected it with their life and anyone who got in their way would be stung. She had to admit that when she thought of those thousands of bees and their stingers, it frightened her.

The two girls stood still and stared at the hive. Sophie asked, "You said you saw a white stone by the hive—do you really think it could be part of the statue?"

"Well, I don't know," Tena, admitted.

"You told me that you had seen something that looked like marble," Sophie said.

"Yes," Tena replied. "But I didn't go and check it out because I saw the hive just a few feet away." She lifted her hands in nervousness. "I thought it was too dangerous. I've heard stories about bees attacking people. I didn't want to go any closer. Maybe it's nothing but a rock, a white rock."

Sophie turned and looked over through the trees. "Let's stay back, but walk around the area of the hive. Let's see if we can find what you saw."

"Alright," Tena agreed, as she walked softly and slowly so she would not disturb the bees.

As they were half way around the hive Tena touched Sophie's shoulder lightly and pointed. Sticking out of the ground was a white stone that did not look like a natural shape to Sophie's eye. From this distance you could not tell whether it was part of the statue or not.

Tena asked, "What are you going to do?" She looked scared. Sophie had never seen Tena look like this before. It made Sophie even more afraid than she already was.

"I have to find out if it's part of the statue. I'm sure that Hestia told me to find the *bees*. Do I trust that or not?" Sophie asked Tena.

She thought, "What if I get close to the hive and they feel me or smell me or whatever it is that bees do? They could attack me, and I wouldn't know where to run or where to go to get away from them. I could endanger Tena, too." She looked down and noticed her hands were shaking.

"Okay," she thought to herself. "Do you believe in the power of the open heart? Do you, really?"

She looked at Tena and said. "I promised to help Wisdom find her body. She said she would help me if I asked. I'm going to sit down and ask her. I want you to stay here and when I'm ready, I'm going to walk close to the hive and look at the stone. I need you to do me a favor, though."

Tena just nodded her head in agreement because the noise of the buzzing bees was so terribly loud. Sophie moved her head so her mouth was close to Tena's ear. "I don't want you to be afraid. I want you to open your heart, too. I need you to be with me. Do you understand?"

Tena nodded her head 'yes' again and her lips mouthed, "I will help you."

Sophie moved back and sat down on the ground. She closed her eyes and tried to stop shaking. She opened her heart, although it took some time to do it because her mind was racing back and forth, telling her to get away from there.

Finally, her mind stopped chattering and she was once again in the Web of Life. She followed her thoughts ... of 'feet'... of 'legs'... and of 'walking'... because she thought that perhaps the stone was the carved portion of Wisdom's feet and legs. She asked for Wisdom's help, and a new connection came forward in her thoughts.

"We use our legs to walk in the world. They carry us into life," she heard inwardly. She asked herself, "Where do I want to go in life?"

Down another thread and around the web she went. "I want to

be someone who makes people's lives better for having known me. I want to make a difference."

"But what about these short legs of mine?" The question loomed large before her. The thread kept moving. It was true, she did not like her short legs. There was no getting around it. Her mother had said she would probably never be a model and it had hurt her feelings. She liked looking at the tall girls at school. Once she had asked Susan, one of her friends, if she liked being tall and she had said, "No, not at all." And Sophie felt sure she had meant it.

Now, a new thought came spiraling into her web. "Well, short legs do not need to hold you back. It is what you do in life that counts, not how long or short your legs are. It is how you walk in life that matters." Then she realized her legs felt stronger just from thinking about them in this new way.

She stopped thinking about stingers and started thinking about honey—sweet, golden honey that she ate each day for breakfast. She thought of her grandfather's celebration this morning with bread and honey.

"Bees live to help each other. They support one another in building and preserving their home.

Bees do not hate, they defend the hive only if someone tries to destroy it." She did not want to hurt any of the bees, and she wanted them to sense that.

Sophie also knew that the Goddess Artemis was helping her with this task right now. "Bees live to serve," she found herself thinking, "I can learn from them as I get ready to walk in the world."

She was prepared for the challenge at hand. Her heart was open and filled with admiration for the bees and for her own journey. After all, you do not see bees fussing over how short or tall they are.

Sophie slowly opened her eyes and got to her feet. She began to hum, low and deep like the bees. Every time she ran out of air, she would take a breath and hum some more.

Sophie hummed and walked and hummed all the way to the stone. She realized the forest was no longer filled with the penetrating sound of the loud buzzing of the bees. Instead, a soft and gentle humming was coming from the hive.

She felt open and filled with respect and love. No bees flew

about her. It was as if they were waiting for something. She realized they were waiting for her.

Sophie looked over at Tena, who was smiling and calmly sitting still. The two of them were working together through their combined focus.

Confidently, Sophie moved to the white stone and bent down. The stone was upside down—that's why she had not been able to tell what it was before. She moved it, guiding it over on its side. Yes! The legs were attached to two impeccable carved feet. There were chisel marks where it had been cut free from its base.

Sophie did not even think about whether or not she could carry it. She lifted it up and walked to Tena, who was now standing ready to help. They walked away from the hive.

Sophie turned and said in a whisper, "Thank you bees. And thank you, Wisdom, for your help." She then spoke louder to Goddess Artemis, "Thank you, my friend."

The girls turned and as they walked farther and farther away from the hive, they heard the familiar humming get louder and louder once again.

Soon, they found a place to rest and took out the brushes that Sophie had brought with her to clean the statue. "We need to clean her feet with water. The brushes will not be enough," Sophie realized. "Is there a stream in this part of the woods?"

"No," Tena said, "but I know where there is a well the shepherds use."

Sophie carried the piece of the statue's legs and feet, and Tena followed, since it was easier to get down the narrow path walking single file. Sophie was careful to focus her thoughts, so that the weight of the piece would not affect her.

Wisdom was walking with her. She was amazed at how tall she felt when she wasn't focused on being too short. For the first time in her life, she felt she was walking with grace.

Chapter 17
Aphrodite and the Well

When the girls reached the well, it looked exactly like Sophie had imagined. Just like the wells she read about in many stories. It was made of large tan stones that had been gathered from the forest. The stones were cemented together, one row on top of another, to form a circular wall around the well. It was located in a clearing, with a large old olive tree not far away. There was an iron bar across the top of the well, with a bucket attached to a thick rope that was used to drop the bucket down into the well to pull up water.

A wooden trough was sitting off to the side where water could be poured and sheep could drink. Sophie took pictures of it. Then she said to Tena, "I feel completely lost and turned around. Where are we?"

Tena gave a little laugh. "Come with me." Sophie had already set the statue down by the well and went with Tena.

To her surprise, she saw that the archeological site was not far away. She remembered how the site had been discovered—after all it was the sheep that found it. As the two friends looked out over a grassy flat area, they could see the temple clearly.

The semi-circle of white statues stood out. Sophie could make out people working and walking about, but could not tell who they were from this distance. The tent was visible and so was the mound, which looked like half a loaf of bread. "I'm glad we're so close to the site. We can take the statue's legs and feet there this afternoon."

They walked back to the well and Tena dropped the bucket down the shaft. She pulled it up by winding the rope around the bar, like a crank.

The water was cold and fresh. They used their hands to cup the water from the bucket and each had a long, refreshing drink. They pulled the statue up to the well and Sophie poured water over it and used her brush to wash it clean. As details of the statue emerged, it was obvious that there was a fissure between the legs and feet. In fact, when Sophie pushed against the fissure, the legs separated into two pieces as if the goddess was ready to move.

Was the goddess giving them another sign? Did they need to hurry? Were they supposed to find more of the statue today?

Sophie was now in deep thought. She sat on the ground with her back against the stonewall of the well. She felt tired, and Tena even asked her if she felt all right. "Yes," she replied. "But I'm sleepy, and I can't explain why."

"Let's go sit under the olive tree while the statue's legs and feet dry here in the sun. That sounded like a terrific idea to Sophie, who felt as if she could barely move.

Tena had brought apples and grapes to eat, so they ate them all and drank more of the good tasting well water, too. Usually, eating would have given Sophie strength, but it did not seem to help. "I think if I lie down and close my eyes for a little bit, I'll feel better," she said.

It was now after twelve o'clock, and they had been in the woods since early morning. They had walked a long way to find the beehive, and even farther to come to the well. So, without even wondering what Tena would do while she closed her eyes, Sophie pulled up her back-pack and laid her head on it and instantly went to sleep.

While she was lying there, she realized there was a noise coming from inside the well. She looked up, and to her surprise a woman was sitting on the edge of the well. Her hair was wet; her complexion was fair and she had delicate features. Her legs were crossed at the ankle, and she was gently swinging her feet from side to side.

Sophie watched the woman reach up and shake out her hair, first on one side and then the other. As the droplets fell, Sophie looked in wonder as they became shiny pearls and bounced on the hard ground around her. The woman smiled a most delightful smile at Sophie. It was friendly and open and Sophie immediately liked her.

The woman asked, "Do you know who I am?" There was a challenge in the tone of voice her.

Sophie thought about the pearls and remembered that when the Goddess Aphrodite had been born, she had come from the sea. She had been born an adult woman, and as she walked across the water of the ocean, pearls had formed from every drop of water that fell from her.

Sophie thought this had to be Aphrodite, so she shouted her name quite loudly, "Aphrodite!"

The woman's face lit up. "So you do know me," she said happily. She slid off the edge of the well and gracefully walked around it. Sophie noticed that wherever she stepped, little flowers sprang to life. Purple, white, and pink violets bloomed with every step she took.

As Aphrodite walked, her dress swayed if she were listening to a melody that only she could hear. She walked over to a low tree branch, shook it, and then bent it off. With no effort at all she made a wreath of fine delicate leaves that she placed on her head. The most curious thing about her, thought Sophie, was that she seemed to glow from within. She was voluptuous and exuded charm, and Sophie thought she was like no one she had ever met.

"I've come to help you, my dear girl," Aphrodite said. "Wisdom has asked me to find her arms and hands, and I've found them for her." She jutted her chin forward and winked.

She looked over her shoulder at Sophie, "Do you know any stories about me?" she asked.

"I've read a few," Sophie replied.

Aphrodite turned around. "Well, don't believe everything you have read about me." A mischievous smile spread quickly across her face.

Sophie had begun to feel better now that Aphrodite was here. She looked around, seeing that Tena was stretched out not far from her, fast asleep. "Don't worry about her," Aphrodite advised. "She is having her own dream about me."

Sophie was startled. "Am I dreaming?"

"Call it whatever you want, but I am here to help you," she responded.

"So, where are the arms and hands of Wisdom?" Sophie asked.

Aphrodite rose up onto her tiptoes, leaned against the well, and with one long finger pointed downward. "Down there," she answered, still smiling.

Sophie was now frowning. If she had to go down that well, this was not going to be a good day.

"Don't worry," Aphrodite said, reading Sophie's thoughts. "You do not have to travel down the well, but you do have to help me get those arms and hands loose. Centuries of mud are piled on top of them down in the well. I will set them free, but the energy I need to be able to do this will come from you."

Sophie began to worry. Aphrodite seemed to be enjoying this entirely too much and explained, "You have to do what you have done each step along the way. You must appreciate your arms and hands in order to free Wisdom's arms and hands."

Next, Aphrodite turned and fluffed her hair some more. She asked, "What do you know about my gifts?"

Sophie replied, "Well, your nature is passionate. Love is associated with you, and also the arts—poetry, dancing, music, and painting."

"So," she said, "close your eyes and get busy. We have work to do. And in case I don't get a chance tell you later, it was a pleasure meeting you, Sophie, and I look forward to the day when we get a chance to meet again."

Sophie closed her eyes, opened her heart, and felt the familiar warm feeling. Since Aphrodite was present, she felt a deeper sense of love moving her to her internal Web of Life. She began looking for the meaning of her hands and arms.

"Well, arms are for reaching. Reaching where?" she asked herself. "Reaching for the best, for the highest, and for the dreams resting inside us." Her words tumbled together as she felt Aphrodite influencing her to keep going.

"But my reach is short," she thought. There they were, those short arms of hers. She thought about how she had not been accepting of them. Then her thoughts turned to drawing and painting. She asked herself whether short arms slowed her down when she was expressing herself. "No, not at all," she thought.

In fact, she realized that if anything, being creative had always helped extend her reach beyond the length of her arms or the size of her hands. "I think I'm getting it."

She laughed to herself and felt her own arms stretch out before her and said aloud, "I love my arms and I love my hands. It is through them that I touch people in all kinds of loving ways."

Thoughts kept tumbling through her. "We can touch people with love. We can use our creativity to celebrate who we are and who we can become."

"My arms and hands are skillful. I love them because they make me a better artist, but I never realized it before." Aphrodite's enthusiasm was contagious. "I accept my creative gifts." Sophie's thoughts were bringing her a feeling of joy.

With that, she sat up, full of energy. Aphrodite was nowhere to be seen. Sophie ran to the well and looked down into the dark water. She saw two white objects sticking out above the top of the water. Those had to be Wisdom's arms down there. She looked at the bucket. It was wide and deep. She looked over at Tena, but she was still dreaming. "This time," she thought, "I need to do it myself."

Sophie unwound the bucket, but steered the rope so it angled in the direction she wanted. She thought of being at the amusement park where you would put money in a machine, and then twist and turn a mechanical arm until you snagged yourself a teddy bear. She was good at that game, and had quite a few bears to prove it.

As she immersed the bucket deep into the well, she heard a 'clink'. "That must be an arm," she thought to herself. Patiently and confidently, she maneuvered the rope to get it exactly where she wanted it. Her arms and hands seemed to move with a freedom she had never felt before.

As if by its own will, the first white arm slipped into the bucket. She worked the crank with one hand and held the rope with the other as it came up. The first marble arm surfaced and she pulled it free from the bucket, carefully putting it down on the ground.

Without delay, she went back to work, lowering the bucket again. Soon, she was pulling the other arm free. As she was placing the second arm on the ground, Tena woke up with a start. Rubbing her eyes, she called out, "Did you see her?"

Sophie secured the bucket and walked over to Tena. "Yes!"

"It was Aphrodite, right?" Tena asked.

"Yes, that's right. She was here at this well," Sophie said.

Tena stood up. "Oh my! I guess I was asleep, but it didn't feel like a dream."

"I know. It felt the same way to me," said Sophie.

Tena saw the arms lying on the ground, and ran over to look at them. "No way! You got them!" She hugged Sophie and shouted, "We have them! We have Wisdom's whole body. Oh, I am so relieved and so happy." She laughed, wiping the tears from her eyes.

She looked at Sophie. "Why aren't you happy like I am?"

"I am happy, Tena. I really am. But I know that I have one more task to do."

"Are you sure? I don't remember anything."

Sophie replied, "Oh, yes, the Goddess of Wisdom was clear. We have to find Wisdom's crown of stars because, without that, the goddess cannot be fully present in our world. I know that when we make her body whole, I have to put her crown on her head. Then, and only then, will the Goddess of Wisdom be alive again."

Now, Tena seemed more serious, but Sophie spun Tena around in a circle, and the two of them danced round and round as fast as they could, laughing all the while. When Sophie stopped, they flew apart and Sophie said, "Let's get these pieces back to the campsite."

The arms had been at the bottom of the well throughout the ages, and now they had to be prepared to come back into the world— so the two of them cleaned the arms and hands of the Goddess of Wisdom.

Tena and Sophie looked around as they prepared to leave the well. Everything was as it had been before. They started to leave, but something sparkling on the ground caught Sophie's eye. She bent down and saw two pearls glistening in the sunlight. She picked them up, putting one pearl in Tena's hand and holding onto the other one. They both took a long look at the pearls. They were flawless and white and filled with subtle rainbow hues. Sophie put hers in her jeans pocket, and Tena did the same.

They looked around, and said in unison, "Thank you, Aphrodite, for your help."

"And," Sophie added, "thank you for the pearls, too."

As they were getting ready to leave they heard the soft laugh of a woman coming up from the bottom of the well.

Chapter 18

The Storm

Sophie was kneeling on a small bench with her arms resting on the window ledge as she leaned out of the window to watch the approaching storm.

The wind had kicked up and the temperature had dropped. The dark sky made it seem like night had come early. The clouds were rolling past, getting darker—changing from deep purple to black as they gathered in the sky.

Sophie reflected on the day as she watched the clouds. The experience of being with the bees was still fresh inside her. And the encounter with Aphrodite at the well had been awesome.

She had bundled, with Tena's help, the statue pieces and tucked them away at the site. She still had Wisdom's face in her closet. It was too delicate to leave at the site just yet.

Continuing to reflect on her day, Sophie was surprised when everyone at the site came up to congratulate her on being right about the identity of Hestia. The statue was half uncovered already and her rounded body had warmth—the kind you would expect your grand-mother to have. The flame in the bowl on the alter was a golden quartz crystal that the artist had sculpted to look like fire. Everyone said that when the sun shone on it the flames glowed.

The professor had shaken Sophie's hand and seemed genuinely excited that Hestia had joined the semi-circle of statues, just as she had predicted. Diane and Beverley came over rather sadly and held out a huge bag filled with all kinds of chocolate. "You have won this fair and square," Diane admitted, but both girls looked hesitant to part with it.

Sophie opened the bag and took out two chocolate squares, handing one to Tena and keeping the other for herself. "Look, you girls need to keep this. You forget Nina cooks for us at the Blue House and I get all the chocolate I want." Sophie had overheard that the graduate students sometimes had a rough time of it.

"This belongs to you," she added. "Thank you, though." The girls looked at each other and Sophie knew they wanted the chocolate back, but were reluctant to take it. Sophie placed the bag in Diane's hand. "It is yours," she said. The two looked at each other, thanked Sophie, and eagerly took back the chocolate.

The wind suddenly blasted past Sophie's face, startling her back from her thoughts about the day's events. Then it seemed that every-thing grew quiet. A few birds flew by heading for cover, and even the insects were silent. All of nature knew that rain was imminent.

Sophie's thoughts returned to the site. She imagined what was probably happening now. The professor and his men were likely dis-cussing where they should take cover when the storm hit. It was too late to cover the exposed statues. The rain let loose in a wall of water. It rained cold and hard. Sophie stuck her hand out the window, and the water hit her hand so hard it hurt. The dusty road by the house turned into a river of mud, and a torrent of water rushed down the hill.

The tile roof above her head rattled loudly as the rain pounded it. Sophie watched as lightning cracked, firing across the sky, and light-ing up the clouds with yellow and white streaks. She imagined every living thing was in its nest or den as the rain poured down.

She thought the best thing for the professor to do was to get in the big heavy Land Rover and ride out the storm. The vehicle was sit-ting in a low area with a wall of solid rocks to one side that would act as a barrier to protect them from the wind if things got too bad. The tent was the last place they ought to be.

Sophie could see the site clearly in her mind's eye. The rain was washing the remaining encasement of soil from the statues of Aphrodite and Hera. The two columns that finished out the semi-circle were also being scrubbed. Nature was rushing through what would have taken the archaeologists several days of hard work to finish. More loud thunder rumbled, and lightening lashed across the sky. Sophie felt safe at her windowsill as she watched Mother Nature bring even more rain.

She felt so close to the statues of the goddesses that in her mind she could see the rain also removing the carpet of earth that still covered the plaka. Nathan, another graduate student, had discovered that a floor of mosaic tiles was beneath the dirt. The tiny squares interlocked to form unique designs across the open plaka. Dirt melted in the downpour and traveled off in little streams, hustling down the hill and harmlessly carrying it to the levels below. Sophie imagined flashes of turquoise color on the floor as the rain washed it clean.

She could not wait to see what it would look like in the morning. Tomorrow, with any luck, the crown of Wisdom would reveal itself, too. For now, she watched nature's show of dazzling light and shimmering rain from the comfort of her bedroom window.

The next day, she and Tena arrived at the site and just as Sophie had imagined, the three statues of the goddesses were completely free of dirt and sand. Hestia was standing tall and bright in the sun. Aphrodite had the same little secret smile on her lips, just like in her dream. And, Hera was gracious and wise, with a trusted peacock at her feet.

The columns were going to need a little more work, but not much. The floor was beautiful with tiles of every shade of turquoise. White spirals were mixed among the tiles, and the effect was as if you were on a rough ocean.

Professor Conrad had weathered the storm in the vehicle, staying there until early morning, when the last of the rain finally stopped. He then inspected everything from top to bottom and was relieved to find all the goddesses unharmed. Sophie thought the goddesses probably knew perfectly well what they were doing with all that rain.

The grad students were cleaning up pools of dirt that remained

on the newly cleared floor. The professor was going to have it pho-
tographed so he could send pictures to his fellow archaeologists in
Athens. More money was going to be needed to preserve what they
had found. It would create a storm of its own when word got out
about the beauty and mystery of this place. Tourists would be coming
in droves. Every day townspeople had already started showing up at
different times to take a look. Who could blame them? It was their
history, and Professor Conrad was always gracious about bringing
people in to see it.

Sophie informed her grandparents that she would be back later
that afternoon. Luckily for Sophie, her grandparents were so excited
about all the changes that had taken place overnight, they agreed to
her being gone until later without giving it any thought.

Sophie and Tena walked past the bundles containing the secret
of Wisdom's body. They checked them, and they were fine. Tena asked,
"How are you going to tell your grandparents about what we found?"

Sophie admitted that she didn't know. "I have to let my intuition guide me. My heart has to show me the way." Then, both girls
turned to leave the site because the crown of Wisdom was calling
them.

Chapter 19
The Cave of Emergence

As they were walking up a stony path they had not followed before, Sophie said, "Let's go back to the meadow. I feel that's the place we are supposed to begin."

She was wondering if the flowers had survived the heavy rain. Once they got there, they were happy to see that flowers were blooming and the meadow was still lovely.

"I'm thinking about the last statue to be revealed at the temple," Sophie said. "It's of Hera, who I learned a lot about when I was researching the discs." She went on, "Hera is attractive, with large amazing eyes. She was famous for having the most beautiful eyes of all the goddesses. She was known as the Queen of Heaven."

"She was well-known for teaching young women how to live better lives. Hera understood how important it was to be a true friend. One who knows how to be kind and shares her dreams and hopes—a friend who supports you when you need help."

"You mean like you and me?" Tena laughed.

Sophie responded, "Yes, like you and me."

Tena just smiled.

They were now walking close to a ledge of rocks. Sophie sat down to rest and drink from her bottle of water. "I asked Wisdom to help us today, and Hera, too. But I haven't seen any sign to tell me whether we are going in the right direction or not."

Without warning, the girls heard a sharp cry that sounded like a wounded bird. "Did you hear that?" Tena asked?

"Yes," Sophie gasped. "It was from over there, I think." She walked closer to some large boulders where a tree leaned out over the stony path.

At first Sophie did not see it, but Tena pointed to the tree. "There."

Sitting balanced on a low limb of the tree was a peacock. "Do you think it's real?" Sophie asked.

"It's hard to say," said Tena. "Hera's symbol is the peacock because of the beautiful-looking eyes in their tail feathers. To the Ancients, the peacock was known as 'the bird with a hundred eyes.'"

"Well, this could be our helper," Sophie said. The girls approached cautiously.

"Have you ever seen a peacock out here in this area?" asked Sophie.

Tena stood still and spoke softly, so as to not frighten the bird. "You're not going to believe this, but I have."

Sophie was surprised. "Where?"

"See that large hill over to the right? A wealthy man has built a grand villa there. He often buys my mother's finest tapestries. He collects weavings from all around the world."

"Just a few weeks ago he invited us to see his villa. He has a huge garden filled with animals and birds. I saw many peacocks that day."

"Do you think this peacock flew over the hill from the villa, coming all this way to find us?"

"Well," Tena said, "I don't know. He would have had to be determined to get here, but I think it's possible."

The bird let out a long, loud cry—so loud that it actually hurt Sophie's ears. "Yikes! You have a shrill voice," she exclaimed. Then he let out another cry—maybe a little louder—to make sure they were paying attention.

Sophie looked intently at the bird, "Did you come from the villa behind this large hill?" The bird, a bit more quietly, sang out as if to say *yes*.

"Have you come to help us?" she asked.

This time, instead of a cry, he jumped down onto the ground. He was a large, fine bird. He raised his tail feathers in a circular array of dazzling beauty. The feathers were iridescent blue and green and gold and they shimmered in the sunlight. He shook the whole frame of feathers.

The girls were impressed. They looked at each other, and Sophie said, "I will take that as a *yes*! Can you show us where to go?"

He shook his feathers again.

Sophie then said to the bird, "You are probably the most beautiful peacock I have ever seen."

That did it. The bird let out a piercing cry, lowered his feathers, and took off flying, going higher than either of the two girls would have thought he could go.

They followed him as he flew. They were on a rugged, stony path and had to climb over rocky formations, often working together to pull one another up. The sun was shining more brightly, and it was getting hot. Once they would get to one level, the peacock would fly up to the next one. On and on they went.

Finally, they made it up the side of the cliff, but both girls had to sit down and rest on a flat area. Sophie looked to the bird and asked, "How much farther?"

But instead of flying away again, the bird jumped down and walked under a group of stones. A small dark opening was visible under one stone. The bird stepped in front of it, but did not go in.

Sophie got up slowly. She had to duck her head to get under the natural ledge that was shading the opening on the side of the rock. She got down on her knees and looked inside. Tena came rushing up. "Wait, don't do anything. That looks like a place for animals to make their home. This could belong to a den of foxes or maybe a snake lives in there."

So Sophie backed up and sat on her knees. She pointed and

looked over at the bird. "That is where I am to go?" she asked. The bird gave a loud cry.

"Great." Tena was not at all convinced that this was a good idea.

"Look," Sophie said, "I'm going to crawl over, lean in, and use my flashlight to look inside."

It was obvious Tena was afraid. She was wringing her hands and looking skeptical. "Okay, be careful."

The bird did not move and Sophie had been counting on his reactions more than she cared to admit. She got out another flashlight and handed it to Tena, who did not want to take it.

Sophie lay on her belly and turned on the light. She peeked in slowly. No animal rushed at her, no growling sound of warning. She crept in a little farther. She could see fairly well in the dark because the light was super bright.

Sophie found herself looking at a small room about as big as her bathroom at the house. She turned and spoke over her shoulder, "I'm going in. It looks empty." She did not wait for Tena's response.

Once inside, she could stand up just fine. Tena shouted, "Are there any bats?"

Sophie aimed her flashlight at the ceiling. "No, I don't see any."

"Okay, then I'm coming in too," and she crawled in on her stomach. Once inside, she stood up and brushed off the dirt with her hands.

With two flashlights it was even easier to be sure that the room was empty. Then Sophie saw a tall thin opening in the wall opposite them. It looked like a doorway. When Sophie went over to it, she felt fresh air moving across her face. It appeared to be an opening to a tunnel. It was so narrow that an adult could not have easily gotten through it, but Sophie and Tena could.

"We have to go through there," Sophie said.

At this thought, Tena shook her head. "No, I'm not going."

Sophie turned to her, "It's okay if you don't want to go, but I have to. You're the one that shared with me about having an open heart. Because of you, I now follow my intuition. Every time I go with my heart I have been safe and have overcome my own fears. If you come with me, it will help me keep my focus. I know I can do it alone, but you decide what you want to do."

Before, Tena's face had reflected intense panic, but now as she listened to Sophie, her face softened. "In other words, I'm not using what I know."

It was Sophie's turn to be the teacher, so she kept opening her heart and finally Tena said, "I know you're right. I felt this way with the bees, and that was just yesterday. I can do this. I can!" At that moment, they heard the peacock make a loud call outside the entrance.

"I think that he agrees," Sophie commented.

Tena smiled, and Sophie knew her friend was going to be okay.

Sophie went first, and they used the flashlights to constantly check the floor and the ceiling. They did not want to walk out onto an empty drop off. The narrow rocky passageway turned right, then left, then right again. The air became stronger and Sophie knew they had reached the end of the tunnel.

Gradually, they entered a huge cave on a ledge that looked safe to walk on. The first thing they noticed was that it was not as dark as they had anticipated. They looked up and saw that a huge section of the cave's ceiling was missing. Daylight streamed down. It was incredibly beautiful. On the floor, directly below the opening was a pool of clear, green water. Next to it, a huge tree grew up toward the light.

Water dripped down from the edges of the opening in the ceiling, splashing and creating magical little circles on the surface of the water. Every drop had a long way to fall. The light made it easier for them to see, but they still needed their flashlights because much of the area was shadowy.

The ledge they were standing on tilted quite steeply, but there was a path that led to the floor below. They used one hand to hold the wall to balance themselves. The wall felt cool and damp. Slowly and deliberately they made their way down to the floor.

They walked closely to the water's edge beside the tree. They thought that a tree in a cave was unusual; yet, there it was.

At the opening in the ceiling, the roots of the hillside trees had grown around it making the whole scene look as if were right out of an enchanted storybook.

They turned and shined their lights on the wall behind them, which looked like it had something on it. Sophie stopped and looked more closely.

At first, she had only seen one handprint, then another, and another, and then more—maybe twenty or so. They were red and black and some were white. She pointed her light higher and gasped in surprise as she realized there were probably at least a hundred handprints on the wall.

The two of them now aimed both of their flashlights higher. No, there were not a hundred handprints; it looked like there were a thousand, maybe more, all concentrated over a particular area on the wall.

"They would have had to use ladders to reach that high," Sophie said. She walked closer, stood on her tiptoes, and put her hand over a red handprint. She saw that it was small, exactly the size of her hand. "Maybe these handprints were made by young girls."

The two girls shined their flashlights on another wall and saw an opening. This one was low to the ground, dark, and small.

Sophie had to bend down on her hands and knees to see it. The bright light of her flashlight shone down a natural tunnel. Then the light touched something reflective. Sophie sprang to her feet, her heart pounding.

"What's wrong?" Tena asked worriedly. "What did you see?" She was quickly moving again into a state of panic.

"No," said Sophie, "it isn't anything to be afraid of. I just need you to take a look to see if we are both seeing the same thing. It's okay. I think I saw something, but I can't be sure of it. Will you just look down the passageway that leads beyond that opening?"

Tena recovered herself, bent low and steadied the light in her hand, and let it travel down the long tunnel. The light hit something that was metal. What it actually was, Tena could not tell. She couldn't see any details on it. She turned to Sophie, "I see it, too. It's metal, I think."

"I have to go in there and look," Sophie announced. "It could be the crown." Tena didn't say anything; she didn't have to.

"This place is ancient—beyond ancient. As though it has been here forever. That's what my feelings tell me," Sophie said intensely.

She looked around now and continued. "My mother who is American-Indian once told me that Mother Nature is all around us outdoors. But she always said that if you want to feel Mother Nature, you have to go inside a cave because it makes you feel as if you are inside her body. This cave is like a cathedral, it must have been sacred to the Ancients who came here."

"Look at that pool of water and the sunlight. I doubt it was like that long ago. This place would have been completely dark, and they would have had to use firelight to see anything." She pointed her flashlight toward the ceiling and shone it on all the handprints. "They all represent people who were once here. They came to pay their respects to Mother Nature. Maybe it was for young girls just like us. The Priestess Iris in the legend knew about this place and she probably brought the crown here to hide it."

Tena listened carefully, then replied, "I think you're right. If it is a crown, what do you have to do before you can go down that tunnel?"

"I have to find out what the crown can teach me," Sophie explained. "I have to earn the right to touch it and, if it is the crown, take it back with us. I'm going to talk out my thoughts with you and follow the Web of Life to see what I discover."

With her eyes open, she began to open her heart, "A crown is a circle. It has no beginning and no end. Kings and Queens have worn them, but the first crown was worn by Wisdom. It had to have meant, for generations of people, that if you wore a crown you were wise like the Goddess of Wisdom."

"Wisdom's crown is made of stars that represent dreams and possibilities." She felt her heart open more as she talked to Tena, and shared wherever the web was taking her.

"I can see now how I've made so many decisions based on how I disliked my looks, or I limited myself because I didn't think I could do something. I felt I wasn't as smart, or as talented, or as athletic as other girls."

"It is not about comparing me to anyone else. It's about finding the things that I love about me, and accepting me just as I am. It's about believing in me. It's about having dreams and knowing that if I have an open heart and listen to wisdom, I'm going to get where I want to go."

Tena was quiet as she listened. Sophie looked at her and said, "Well, I'm ready now. I'm going to go and get her crown."

She had to get down on all fours to move through the small dark tunnel. She paused at the entrance. It was going to be tight. She turned on her flashlight and held it in one hand. Tena perched herself beside the entrance and added her light to Sophie's.

Sophie took a deep breath and began crawling. She focused her mind by thinking how sacred this place must have been. Perhaps many girls had gone through this tunnel. Maybe it was a 'rite of passage' to show that they could one day grow up to be wise women. Today, Sophie's purpose for going through this tunnel was to restore Wisdom to the world and to herself.

Sophie crawled forward slowly until she reached a small outcropping of rocks. At one time, something would have been placed on it. Whatever it had been, it was gone now. But there in its place, in golden glory, sat the crown.

Sophie's hands trembled, not because she was afraid, but because she was hypnotized by actually seeing the crown. She gently picked it up and held it to her heart. She had to crawl backwards to get out of the tunnel, but it went much faster than coming in.

When she got to the opening, Tena was waiting anxiously for her. Sophie backed all the way out holding the crown, sat up on her knees, and took a deep breath. She had done it!

She felt excited and light in spirit—like she could do absolutely anything now. She imagined all the girls who had gone before her through that tunnel in the dark. She wished she could put her handprint on the wall, too.

As they examined the crown they knew they were holding an amazing piece of art. It was a circular band of gold with a large star in the middle representing Sophia, the Goddess of Wisdom. Attached to the band were seven smaller stars, symbolizing the seven goddesses.

Through the stillness they heard a familiar cry from high in the trees outside the cave opening. The peacock had never left them. Its mission now done, they saw it fly away. "Our guardian was with us the whole time," Sophie said.

"Are you ready to leave?" Tena asked.

"Piece of cake," she replied. "Let's go."

They both giggled, holding Wisdom's crown, ready to bring it into the light.

Chapter 20

The Feast

Early the next morning, Sophie left the Blue House before her grand-parents had awakened. She carried her canvas bag under her arm heading toward the site. The fog had come in that morning and the place had an eerie feeling about it, as if she were going back in time. In many ways today, she was.

Tena was meeting her at the site; they both wanted to be there before anyone else arrived. She had learned that the professor had to go to his vineyard the night before and would not be back until morning.

The graduate students would be arriving with Nikos, so they would not arrive at the site until at least an hour from now. Her grand-parents were still at home. They would get her note about the time Nina got there, and would be curious that she had gone to the site before them. They would arrive just about when Sophie wanted them to, if her plan held together.

The afternoon before, Sophie had Tena translate for her telling the guards that she was going to come early the next morning before anybody else got there. She had Tena explain that she was doing some special photography for a school project. To her surprise, the guards accepted the idea completely. They would expect to see her in the morning, no problem.

What Sophie had to do now felt harder than anything else she had done before. Yes, she had gathered together all the parts of Wisdom's body for the purpose of restoring her to the world. She also knew that in the field of archaeology, she had completely disobeyed all the rules.

She had retrieved each part without documenting it with photographs taken in its original location. She had not measured one piece of the statue, either. The biggest issue was that all the pieces were found in different locations—making it difficult to prove they were all from the same statue. She had proposed no theory about the statue, and had not asked permission to bring the pieces back to the site by herself, let alone asking Tena, another twelve-year-old girl, to help her.

She had to explain to them that everything she had done was because of a dream that showed her what to do. She had followed her *intuition*, a word she had never heard anyone of them use. If that did not qualify her as crazy, nothing would.

This was the restoration, not just of a statue, but of Wisdom herself. She kept asking the goddess to help her, because she knew she was going to need it.

When Sophie got to the site, it was coated with a thick mist. She pulled the camera from her backpack and reintroduced herself to the guards. They just waved as they gathered around the hot coffee pot. She took a few pictures and went to get two large canvas tarps. She put one down on the ground next to the platform of the missing statue.

Tena came walking up and scared her as she emerged silently out of the mist. "How did you get here so fast?" she asked.

Tena just gave her a wicked little smile and said, "I flew here."

"Okay, come on," Sophie answered back, more than a little stressed. "Let's get the statue pieces."

The two girls used the powers of focus one more time as they lifted each of the bundles and walked them over to the canvas and placed them on the ground. They untied everything and, one by one, arranged the pieces. First, the two pieces with the feet and legs were put in place. Second, the torso and the two arms were placed. Lastly,

Sophie took the head of Goddess Sophia out of her bag and placed it close to, but not touching, the neck. It was the first time the girls had seen all the pieces together. It gave them both a thrill.

Sophie left the crown in the bag. She had polished it the night before and had actually left it on her bed so she could look at it all night. It wasn't every day that you had Wisdom's crown in your bedroom.

Now that it was all arranged correctly, they covered it over with another canvas and set about waiting until everyone arrived. While she waited, Sophie took pictures of each statue one more time. The mist added a wonderful feeling of timelessness to each image. They were like friends to her now, not just marble statues.

As the sun came out, the mist and fog gradually disappeared, the camp slowly returned to life. Everyone seemed to arrive within a few minutes of each other. Sophie and Tena were sitting on the side of the hill in a place they could easily see everyone gathering.

Sophie was the first to realize that they were all getting together in the tent, probably for some kind of meeting. The workers were all waiting to see what, if anything, they would be doing that day.

Sophie opened her heart and waited until she felt the familiar feelings. She knew her intuition would tell her when to go to the tent. Soon, she stood up feeling the pull to go. To herself she whispered, "We are not separate, we are *all* connected."

She entered the tent where the professor was standing and talking. But the minute she came in, all eyes turned to her. She put her arms behind her and clasped her hands. They waited for her to speak, then she began, "I'm sorry to interrupt you, but I feel I have something important to share."

No one said a word, not even her grandparents. "What I have to share with you is over on the plaka where the missing statue is located. Would you come there with me?" She half expected that they would need convincing. However, the idea that a twelve-year-old girl was asking all of these adults to follow her must have been so unusual that when the professor said, "Okay, let's go," they all stood up quietly and followed her without saying a word.

Next, she saw the workers join them, and then Nikos and the guards who were getting ready to leave came over. "Great!" Sophie thought, "I wonder who else will show up." She tried to stay focused and not be nervous.

Just at that moment everyone's attention was drawn to an awful noise being made by a car. It snorted and banged its way up the small driveway at the end of the site when someone blurted out, "It's Nina and George." They got out of their old car and Sophie thought for sure the doors were going to fall off as they slammed them shut.

Nikos went to meet them, and in less than a minute Nina and her husband stood looking at her, too. She composed herself and stood as tall as she could. She spoke strongly, "I have something to show you." Sophie signaled to Tena, and the two of them lifted the canvas tarp off the pieces of the statue lying underneath it. A rush of excitement went through the group. But, Sophie could see that no one was connecting the dots or understood exactly what they were looking at.

"These," she proudly informed them, "are the pieces of the missing statue." Now, all at once, they got it. The air erupted with spontaneous talking—the workers and guards in Greek, and everyone else in English.

Someone said, "You've got to be kidding." "Look at the face."

Sophie's grandmother bent down to look more closely, but in a few minutes all eyes were on Professor Conrad.

He stood near the middle of the display of marble pieces. It was clear that he was experiencing a whole range of feelings. One part of him was upset, probably even angry. Why hadn't he been told about this? Who had given the girls permission to do this? They definitely had not followed the rules. And where had all these pieces come from?

Then his face reflected the *other* part of himself. Could it be true? The missing goddess *found?* He had devoted his whole life to finding something worthy of sharing with humanity. He had been involved with the best archaeological project of his life. He had found a fabulous treasure in this temple complex, and he intended that the world would benefit by seeing it. Now he could finish it, make it complete. The girls had given him an extraordinary gift. He should be happy.

Sophie and everyone watched his face. They could see his emotions and thoughts were in total agitation. What was he going to do?

Sophie went over to the bag she had brought with her and reached inside. She carefully pulled out the golden crown. As the bright sunlight struck the surface, it lit up like it was on fire. It gleamed and glittered in her hands. *Now* everyone seemed to go crazy with excitement. "Wow!" "Awesome!" "Do you see that?" Can you believe it?" "Is it a crown?" "Is that gold?"

Once again, everyone was talking at the same time. Sophie did not hesitate. She knew what to do next. She handed the crown to Professor Conrad.

He took it without thinking, for his mind was filled with the golden stars now dancing in his hands. He turned it this way and that. He looked at it with his professional eye. The confusion still raged inside him. Then, Sophie saw it—a flicker like someone was igniting a match.

Deep in his eyes, she saw it turn on. Wisdom had ignited inside him. Sophie spoke clearly, "I want to share a dream I had—a dream about restoring the body that now rests at our feet." She continued, "I believe that this is not just the body of a marble statue. It represents the body of the Goddess Sophia, the body of Wisdom. I would like Professor Conrad, if he can, to rebuild her body and restore her to us."

The professor looked at her. His anger subsided. "I don't know how I will explain all of this but I will find a way. There is no question we must restore her body." He spoke with deep conviction in his voice.

With that, a triumphant shout went up from everyone at once. The energy of the excitement descended on everybody. It was so powerful it rippled through the entire group.

One of the workers stepped forward. She spoke quietly, and everyone stopped to listen. "Sir," she said to the professor, "my name is Christina and I was trained in Italy to restore antique marble statues like this one. I am, sir, if I may say so, an expert. I have been working here because I felt drawn to this place. I have everything at my house I need in order to work with this beautiful statue. My house is only ten minutes away."

The professor listened and then clapped his hands together loudly. "Yes! Let's restore the statue of Wisdom today. Let's do it!" The crowd went wild, and all the students were down on their knees looking at the pieces of the statue.

Above the din of voices, Sophie's grandfather yelled, "I think we need to have a Feast of Celebration!"

Sophie saw Nina slip over to her grandparents and say something. As Nina broke out into a big smile, she said, first in English and then in Greek, "I know where to get the food for our feast."

Nikos and Nina's husband headed for the van and the Blue House. Christina ran to her truck to go get her supplies. The workers and guards moved swiftly to the tent, bringing tables and chairs over to the plaka where the food would soon be laid out.

Sophie's grandparents looked at the crown the professor was holding. Tena came over and whispered into Sophie's ear, "When are you going to tell them the dream?"

"When the statue is put together," she said. The girls walked away a bit and sat down on the grass. Everyone was scurrying about, and the place was filled with life.

Sophie took Tena's hand in hers, "I need to tell you something, because when this day is finished I might not have a chance to say this. Tena, you have been the best friend a girl could ever have. Goddess Hera is right; the greatest gift a person can give another is true friendship. You stood by me, encouraged me, taught me how to see and feel the world in a new way. I cannot imagine how I could tell you more clearly what you have meant to me." Sophie's eyes had grown moist.

Tena took in all of what Sophie had said and smiled a faint smile of modesty. "Sophie, you are my dear friend, and we will never forget this incredible adventure we have been on. When I was back at the beehive, I was so afraid. And," she laughed, "when I was at the cave I was even more frightened. You became my teacher, and you helped me, too. You helped me feel like I could do anything."

The two girls hugged each other fondly. Their friendship would always be strong.

Nikos and Nina's husband were back. They watched as Nina carried an abundance of food to the tables. Dishes of roasted chicken and lamb, baskets of freshly baked breads, fruits, cheeses, olives, spanakopita, and even baklava for dessert was all spread out for everyone to enjoy.

Tena asked Sophie, "Did you see the professor back there? He looked pretty upset at first."

"Yes, I think he got caught up in all of the rules and regulations, and the way things *should* have happened," Sophie said. "But, when he held Wisdom's crown in his hands, it seemed that his heart softened and he understood everything."

She then stood up. "We still have one more thing to do, Tena."

"Do you think we could eat first?" Tena suggested, her stomach growling.

Sophie laughed. "Now, you sound like my grandfather." Sophie started to move toward the tables. "Yep, I think we need to eat. I think we need to eat a lot!"

Sophie's grandparents at one point had come over to her and told her how proud they were of what she had accomplished. They were immensely moved by what was going on. Sophie told them how grateful she was that they had brought her to Greece. The love they had for one another had grown even stronger.

The feast continued and Christina had brought her husband, Joe, and their two little boys back with her so they could all watch her work on the restoration. She had begun to mix her compounds together and, with six workers helping her, the feet/leg sections were soon put in place on the pedestal. Sophie smiled at the thought that she alone had carried it to the site—with Wisdom's help, of course.

Once the feet were in place, a cheer went up that was so loud it hurt Sophie's ears. Christina worked like a conductor of an orchestra and everyone moved in harmony with one another. She knew what she was doing and she did it well.

Later, after everyone had eaten, including Christina and the other workers, the crowd grew silent. The workers' wives and husbands had appeared with more children and townspeople. Tena's mother, Métis, came, too. Most everyone sat on the ground as the statue came together layer by layer, like a birthday cake. "Wisdom's birthday," Sophie thought.

Sophie had understood that there were seven parts to Wisdom's body. There were her two feet/legs pieces, which were now joined to the third part, the torso. With them joined together, you could see how the dress of marble flowed. The arms were the fourth and fifth parts, and everyone watched as one arm went on, and then another. Magically, it all held together.

The crowd grew larger as Christina fused the lovely face/head, the sixth part, to her neck. It was a triumphant moment once the head was in place.

The seventh part would be the crown, which Sophie knew

Chapter 20

would activate Wisdom's journey back into the world. It would also awaken the seven goddesses who stood behind her.

Sophie's heart was filled with joy. The best was yet to come.

Chapter 21
Wisdom Comes Back into the World

All eyes now seemed to drift back to Sophie. The air was warm, but not hot. Long thin clouds drifted on the horizon in the sky. Something invisible gathered in the air above them and waited.

Professor Conrad stood up, "Sophie, I don't know how you and Tena did this. I hope sometime you will tell me the rest of the story. I have the feeling it wasn't easy. I think I speak for all of us when I say that we are grateful to you and Tena for unifying the power of this temple once again. I know the Ancients wanted us to find all of this, and I feel them here today."

Sophie's grandmother, who was holding her grandfather's hand, chimed in, "We are proud of both of you girls." There was a gentle laugh from the group. The graduate students waved, and her friends Beverley, Diane, and Robert were smiling and genuinely excited for her.

Then Professor Conrad said, "Sophie, would you do us the honor of telling the rest of your story?"

Chapter 21

Sophie stood up confidently. She felt tall as she walked over to where the crown had been placed on the table. As she picked it up, a hush fell over the crowd.

She said with strength in her voice, "I would like to offer you the opportunity to hold this crown before I place it on Wisdom's head." She handed it to Christina first.

Sophie then walked over to stand by Tena and her grandparents. "I will tell the story of my dream now." Several people began to quietly translate her words for those who did not understand English.

She watched the crowd while she spoke and noticed that when each person held the crown, a light of awareness flickered in their eyes. Wisdom was opening their hearts and their minds.

By the time she finished telling her dream, everyone had had the chance to hold the crown. She glanced around and saw that birds now filled every branch of every tree around the site. There were owls and doves, and even birds she had never seen before. And, of course, at the front was her peacock friend standing with his mate beside him. She saw deer and fox, and many animal eyes were peering out from behind the trunks of trees. Even the trees seemed to be listening and waiting. All had been called to be witness to Wisdom's return.

Then the insects, including the cicadas and the locusts, began to sing. Louder and louder, like a choir of voices, they rubbed their wings together to create nature's symphony.

Sophie's grandfather stepped forward and motioned for her to come over. Carefully, she took the crown from the last little girl standing in the crowd. She looked around and saw the crowd had been transformed. Wise people were staring back at her without fears or limitations. Tears started to roll down Sophie's cheeks.

Her grandfather, filled with strength he normally did not possess, lifted Sophie up so she could reach Goddess Sophia's head. As Sophie placed the crown on her head, she proclaimed, "I, Sophie, Born Goddess, return you Wisdom to the world, and from this day forward I shall be called, Sophia."

The golden crown of stars fit perfectly as it slid into place. Her grandfather gently set her back down on the ground. The insects stopped singing and an electrical current ran through the crowd. Everyone could feel it.

Wisdom Comes Back into the World

Young Sophia was the first to see the light that swirled behind Wisdom's statue—a pure, golden light.

A shower of tiny stars began at the same time to move around the ground, sweeping upward, flying all around the statue and up into the sky. The marble was then replaced by a being of golden light.

Goddess Sophia shook herself free of her constraints. Her hair fell loose, and her gossamer gown floated down to the ground around her. She lifted her arms, stretched her fingers, and laughed a magical laugh of a thousand crystal bells. Young Sophia looked at the crowd and could see in their faces the awe in seeing the goddess come to life.

The stars of the goddess' golden crown glittered with light. She stepped down to the ground, and the crowd opened to give her room. Her presence was love itself, and a deep reverence fell upon everyone for they saw and knew that Wisdom did exist. The Goddess Sophia walked out onto the plaka. She moved like a dancer across the turquoise and white mosaic tiles, lightly and joyfully. Young Sophia followed, as did Tena and everyone else.

Goddess Sophia spread her arms and lifted them skyward. Currents of electricity crackled through the air. The seven goddesses behind her, who stood so delicately carved, seemed to tremble with anticipation. Goddess Sophia's stars seemed to connect to each one of them, and in a few moments each goddess was alive and radiant. They were dazzling to look at.

The goddesses looked around and smiled at each other. Although they had once been in the world, people had forgotten them. They could easily have faded away forever. But now they had been renewed by Wisdom's grace. They saw each other, and joy filled the plaka. They were truly sisters. They came to Goddess Sophia, and they all held hands and kissed each other on the cheeks. It was a sight never to be forgotten.

Wisdom turned to the people, "I am the Goddess Sophia, who is Wisdom. I have returned to bring the wisdom of my sisters back into the world to help you. I live in them, and they in me. Please receive our gifts and call upon us to guide you. Remember, an open heart is open to us."

With those words, a sweet surge of voices stirred among the people as they grew bright with hope and excitement. Anything could be possible now.

Chapter 21

The Goddess of Wisdom said, "Because young Sophia has been willing to face her fears and limitations to bring me back into the world, and because Tena walked the journey with her, growing and deepening Sophia's life with hers, I have an extraordinary gift for them."

She looked at the two girls standing together. "Give me the pearls of Aphrodite." Each girl pulled a single white pearl from her pocket.

"Place them in my hands," the goddess said. And, the girls did. The goddess went on to explain, "The pearl is a symbol of my Wisdom. It starts out as a mere grain of sand." She smiled, and young Sophia thought her heart would burst it was so filled with love. "Then it becomes a pearl." She closed her fingers around the pearls and raised her hands high in the air. She closed her eyes as if to concentrate and, a few moments later, brought her arms back down to her sides. She opened a hand to each girl. Inside each was a golden ring attached to Aphrodite's pearl. Inside the band was written, *Born Goddess.*

"Take these. If you need me, I will be present to you anywhere." Each girl picked up a ring and placed it on her finger. They could not help but beam with delight.

Then, Goddess Sophia said to the girls, "Now, I know all my sisters want to meet both of you." With that, the seven goddesses walked over to the girls and embraced them.

First, Athena came—bold, strong, and golden in her armor. She pulled her helmet off her head and set it on the ground. She took Tena's hands speaking only to her, "You are my light. You are my reflection in the world because we share the same name. Know that you are a *Born Goddess.* From now on you will be known by your full name, Athena.

Young Sophia thought at that moment, seeing them together, that it was like they were two halves of a whole. Young Athena was the friend with whom she had shared these adventures. Now, she seemed to be so much more. Whatever was happening, young Athena's face was beaming with love from the goddess.

With her other hand, Goddess Athena reached out to young Sophia. She drew her closer. "I saw you first when you came to my home in the Parthenon. Remember how I nodded my head to you?"

"Yes," young Sophia whispered.

"I was letting you know that I believed in you. You have been brave and true and strong."

Athena stood tall, and for the first time young Sophia saw that her owls were gliding in the air high above her. She swept her hand out as if addressing not only the girls, but everyone and said: *I give you the gift of Leadership!*

Artemis now sprinted forward. She glowed with the beauty of nature around and inside of her. Her short kilt gently settled at her knees. Her quiver of silver arrows was strapped to her back, and she looked athletic and fit. Two stags strode in from behind her. She stroked each one's head and sent them back to the edge of the woods where all the other deer stood watching her with keen alertness.

Artemis raised her hands in a playful way. "Moonlight becomes us." At that moment, it became night and a huge full moon hung in the sky. The crowd let out a collective gasp of astonishment.

Artemis looked at young Athena and took her hand. "You both have been kind to my animals and respectful to my bees."

She turned and took young Sophia's hand, too. "You girls are most welcome in my woods any time of day or any season." She looked into young Sophia's eyes and said, "I delight in you." Young Sophia once again felt fullness in her heart. Then Artemis said boldly to all: *I give you the gift of Independence!*

Next, Demeter rushed over to meet the girls. Her daughter, Persephone, followed closely behind. Demeter took both girls and hugged them to her body. Warmth and motherly love poured out of her as her cloak of green satin swirled around both girls. "You girls are my daughters, too," she said lovingly. Young Athena looked across at young Sophia, and all she could do was smile. It felt so good.

With a slight skip in her step, Persephone then stepped forward, at first a little shy. "It was fun to be with both of you in the meadow. Did you like my little earthquake?"

'Oh, yes," young Sophia replied. "Without it we would never have found Wisdom's body."

Persephone chuckled. "I, too, am proud of you and all you accomplished for us." She tenderly looked into her mother's eyes and smiled.

Demeter addressed the girls and all the people: *I give you the gift of Kindness and Generosity!*

Chapter 21

Persephone stood tall as the Queen she was and said: *I give you the gift of Intuition and Imagination!*

Swiftly, Hestia approached the two girls and burst into flames of red, violet, blue, and gold that danced inside her presence. Her large body was welcoming, and her deep warmth made them feel safe. The scent of cedar and pine and wisps of smoke drifted around her. It made for a lovely perfume. Her voice was soft and light. "Oh, I am thrilled to see you girls again. I am the Goddess of Transcendence and Centeredness. Through me you can find the quiet place in your heart where you can hear wisdom. Remember, I live in the flame and if you should ever need me—that is where you'll find me." In an instant, she burst into flames again and made herself burn brightly, full of colors and sizzling sparks and said: *I give you the gift of the Centeredness!*

Aphrodite gracefully walked forward. She moved so elegantly, it was as if she were dancing. The ground at her feet was instantly covered in spring flowers, and more grew wherever she stepped. Her laughter was impossible to resist, and her charm and playful nature made you want to spend all of your time with her. She turned to the girls, smiling, "We had quite a good time at the well that day, didn't we? You must come visit my home where I was born, for the sea is an enchanting place to be. I look forward to working with you again."

She bent down and picked two flowers from the earth and gave one to young Sophia. At once, it turned into a paintbrush. She then gave the other flower to young Athena, which immediately transformed into an abalone shell pen. "Create, girls! And tell our stories well." With a flourish, she adjusted her lovely hair and announced: *I give you the gift of Creativity!"*

Dressed in a sky-blue tunic, and every inch a queen, the tall and stately Hera walked up to the girls with her peacocks at her feet. She clasped each girl by the hand and kissed their cheeks. "I love all girls and women," she said. "There are so many things to learn in the world, and I love to teach all that I know, especially the gift of friendship. It will be wonderful to share my knowledge again."

The light in her face made it obvious. She was so alive and awake and gracious and regal. Young Sophia just loved her, as did young Athena. They were reluctant to let go of her hands, but she winked at them and said: *I give you the gift of Friendship!*

Wisdom then looked at her sisters, each bathed in the magical light of the moon. Aphrodite rushed forward, "In Greece, one of the finest gifts a girl can receive is a koukla, or doll. We want you both to remember the magnitude of this day and to continue to share what you have learned with girls everywhere. So, we have decided to give each of you seven kouklas that represent us and our gifts."

Each goddess held out her hands. Pink and green and purple and orange fire danced across the plaka. At each girl's feet, the kouklas appeared—seven of them, each one looking exactly like one of the goddesses.

Young Sophia and young Athena bent down and gathered them up, holding them to their hearts.

Then the Goddess of Wisdom turned and looked to each person and to the girls. All seven of the goddesses stood beside her. They raised their arms and, with the palms of their hands open, said as one voice: *We are Wisdom, we are alive, seek us!*

At this decree, all the owls and doves and other birds flew into the air at once. The earth seemed to shimmer with promise and the hope of dreams. Energy flowed and sparkled as a wind rose up and carried all the goddesses into the air. Their radiance filled the night sky. Then they burst into a million points of light, showering down upon the earth as they traveled to places far and wide, to every corner of the world. For this day, Wisdom lived once again.

Everyone began to celebrate at once. People sang and danced and hugged each other. They were not strangers anymore. The secret was known—they were not separate, but connected to one another.

The temple remained glowing in the moonlight, evidence of the Ancients touching the future. "No doubt," young Sophia thought, "many people will remember this night as if it were a dream—a dream they will not soon forget."

As for young Sophia and young Athena, they looked at each other and smiled. They *knew* it was real. Young Sophia gazed up at the glorious moon now shining high above them in the sky. Tonight she did not see the man in the moon. Instead, she saw Wisdom's gentle face smiling down on them.

Glossary

abalone shell	A one-piece coiled shell; the colorful pearly interior is often used for making ornaments
Acropolis	A hill rising high above Athens
amidst	Surrounded by or in the middle of something
analogy	A comparison between things that have similar features
Ancients	People who lived hundreds or even thousands of years ago
anticipation	To imagine or expect that something will happen
archaeology	The study of the buildings, tools, and other objects that belonged to people who lived in the past
archaeologist	Someone who studies archaeology
artifacts	Objects of archaeological or historical interest
avalanche	A large amount of dirt or rock quickly falling down
broken English	Limited use of the English language by foreigners
cascade	To hang down or flow over an object

centeredness	The skill of focusing at your heart center and placing thoughts and emotions aside or on hold—you become independent of outside forces and influence
cicada	A large insect found in warm countries that produces a high continuous sound
compassion	A strong feeling of sympathy and sadness for the suffering or bad luck of others with a desire to help them
contemplate	To spend time considering a possible future action, or to consider one particular thing for a long time in a serious and quiet way
crescent	A curved shape that has two narrow pointed ends, like the moon when it is less than half of a circle
crevice	A small narrow crack or space
debris	Broken or torn pieces of something larger
Delphi	Home or location of the Delphic Oracle
depicted	To represent or show something in a picture or story
dilemma	A situation in which a difficult choice has to be made between two different things
encasement	Something that is covered or enclosed
encasing	To cover or enclose something or someone completely
entwined	Closely connected or unable to be separated

eons	A period of time that is so long, it cannot be measured
Erechtheum	A temple in Athens on the Acropolis
excavate or excavation	To remove earth; a place that covers very old objects buried in the ground in order to discover things about the past
exquisite	Very beautiful and delicate
exuded	To give off something
fissure	A deep narrow crack in rock
geometric	Describes a pattern or arrangement that is made up of shapes such as squares, triangles, or rectangles
Gia Gia	Greek for grandmother
Hades	King of the Underworld in Greek mythology
hues	A degree of lightness, darkness, or strength of color
imminent	Something likely to occur at any moment
insight	A clear, deep, and sometimes sudden understanding of a complicated problem or situation
intense	Extreme or very strong, especially in feeling
intervene	To become involved in a difficult situation in order to improve it

intuition	An ability to understand or know something in your body without needing to think about it, learn it, or discover it
magnitude	Greatness or importance
matador	A bullfighter
mind's eye	A very clear picture in your mind of how something can look or how an idea can be used
monumental	Exceptionally great, as in quantity or quality
mysterious	Unusual without explanation or understanding
mythology	A series of stories associated with a culture
Nike the Goddess of Victory	Goddess who presided over all contests, Athletic as well as military
nuance	A small difference in meaning, opinion, or attitude
oracle	A female who gives people wise advice
Pa Pou	Greek for grandfather
Parthenon	A temple in Greece
plateau	An elevated level piece of land
plummeted	To fall straight down

pomegranate	A fruit having many seeds with juicy red pulp in a tough brownish-red rind
ponder	To reflect or consider with thoroughness and care
plaka	Greek for plaza
radiance	The quality of being bright and sending out rays of light
rapt	Deeply absorbed in something mentally
reflect (as a mirror)	To give back or show an image
reflective (introspective)	Deep or serious in thought
reluctant	Unwilling or hesitant to do something
repelled	Pushed or driven away
rite of passage	A ritual or ceremony that marks a change in a person
scholars	People who have studied a long time and have gained mastery at something
site	The place where a structure or group of structures are or have been
surreal	Having a dreamlike quality
tapestry	A heavy cloth woven with rich, colorful scenes
three-dimensional	Having depth, as well as width and height
timelessness	Unaffected by time; ageless
transcendence	A state of being above and beyond the limits of real experience

virtue	A good or admirable quality
voluptuous	Having a well-proportioned and pleasing shape
vulnerable	Being emotionally open and capable of being hurt or criticized
Web of Life	How all living things in our environment are connected
wisdom	Opens our heart and lets the spirit of Sophia/Wisdom guide our actions to a greater sense of good—it is also the ability to use knowledge and experience to make good decisions and judgments
Yasoo	Greek for hello
Zeus	King of the gods, ruler of Mount Olympus, and god of the sky and thunder in Greek Mythology

Parent Guide

This book is the story of a girl's journey into self-acceptance. After sharing this adventure with those special girls in your life as a mother, grandmother, aunt or wise friend—together discuss and discover an easier, more entertaining way to understand the basic tools of self-esteem uncovered in this book.

The lesson of WISDOM: refer to the story and discuss how Sophie learned to use her wisdom to make small and difficult decisions.

Note: Just as Sophia, the Goddess of Wisdom, shared her knowledge with Sophie, this is an opportunity to share thoughts on how wisdom may be used to make better choices in life.

The concept of being BORN GODDESS: refer to the story and discuss the characteristics of the goddesses (wise, kind, intelligent, creative, and with few limitations).

Note: Unlike a queen or a princess (who rules over subjects or depends on a prince to save her), the goddesses interact with others and share knowledge and compassion while promoting independence. This is an opportunity to discuss heritage, which defines our viewpoints of physical, emotional, and spiritual understanding. Goddess attributes offer an opportunity to break through old thought patterns and discover the true powers within each of us.

The discovery of true SELF-ACCEPTANCE: refer to the story and discuss the importance of Sophie's commitment to finding the parts of each goddess and "putting it together" for a complete beautiful statue.

Note: The Goddess of Wisdom, in asking Sophie to locate the pieces of her statue, teaches her the acceptance of her body features and innate gifts. Share how this type of self-discovery leads to a happier and more fulfilled life.

Exercises

Here are some exercises that reinforce the main message of the book—self-acceptance. Most of the exercises are easy and shouldn't be forced. Besides, it will be fun to do them together. This is a wonderful way to identify some areas where you need encouragement. It's important for all girls to know they are *Born Goddesses,* just like Sophie and Tena.

Exercise #1—Chapter 8

Sit quietly with your mother beside you—you may also do this exercise alone. Close your eyes and breathe slowly, then ask your mind to slow down as you try to focus on your heart. Place your hand on the center of your chest to help you slow down your breathing and thinking. Now, think about someone you love: your grandmother, mother, father, best friend, your pet, or even your favorite place. Let that feeling of love grow stronger inside of you.

Pay attention so that you will be able to feel the love in your heart. Let this feeling grow as your heart center becomes warmer and stronger. Open your eyes and become aware of how wonderful you feel. Anytime you are not feeling good or something has gone wrong in your day, practice doing the heart exercise for just a few seconds. Listening to your heart will help you become a young girl of wisdom, just like Sophie and Tena.

Exercise #2—Chapter 12

Since scrap-booking is popular, create a page in your scrapbook that you can call your "Heritage Page." Place a picture of yourself in the middle of the page. Next, glue pictures of your family around your picture. Study each picture for a few seconds. Who do you look like? Do you have any similar features? Do you share a particular smile, hairline, or a certain look in your eyes? Remember to appreciate everything about you—it's your heritage.

Exercise #3—Chapter 14

Step 1 – Stand up and raise your strongest arm straight out to the side of your body so that it is parallel to the ground. Now, think a negative thought that creates a negative feeling about your body—something you do not like about your body. While holding onto this negative thought and feeling, ask your mother to lightly press down on this strong arm to test your resistance—if your arm moves downward, your thinking and emotions are affecting your body. Discuss this feeling with your mother and remember how that negative energy felt in your body.

Step 2 – Think of something that creates a positive feeling about your body—something you like about the way you look. While holding onto this positive thought and feeling, say out loud that you want your body to feel like Sophie's when she appreciated her body.

Exercise #4—Chapter 14

Here is an affirmation you might want to say every morning before getting out of bed and just before you go to sleep, "I love and accept my body just as it is." Say these words as often as you like and with plenty of love for yourself. Now, ask your mother to press down on the strong arm again and see if, this time, your arm does not move.

Note how much stronger you feel inside your heart when you are thinking and feeling good things about your body. You may want to ask your mother if she would like to try this exercise, too, with you helping her. It may be fun and helpful for you both.

Exercise #5—Chapter 16

Ask your mother to think about being happy and proud of who she is. Have her to think those thoughts for at least 30 seconds, while you count. Next, ask your mother to walk across the room with these good feelings in her heart. Can you tell what she is thinking by the way she walks? Now, it's your turn. Think about something you did recently that made you feel good about yourself, then, walk across the room like your mother. How does this feel? Do you have similar feelings or did you walk the same way? Spend some time talking about this.

At another time, try the following exercise. Walk in ways that express your different moods such as happy, angry, proud, excited, afraid, and sad. Then, ask your mother if she can see the difference in the way you walk. Let her guess which mood you are "walking." Now, when you feel angry, afraid, or sad, remember to walk the way you felt when you "walked" happy, proud, and excited.

Exercise #6—Chapters 17

Sophie realized that her creativity could help her reach beyond her limitations. Create something with your creative imagination that you have never made before. Remember, creativity exists in many ways: painting, cooking, sewing, gardening, writing, etc. You decide. Use your creative arms to reach out and help someone right now. Here are some ideas:

Design a greeting card and tell a special person in your life how much you love and appreciate him or her.

Bake some cookies and give them to someone who is lonely and needs a friend.

Sew or mend something that can be useful to another and give it to them.

Arrange some flowers in a bouquet and deliver them to a person in need.

Exercise #7—Chapter 17

Make a list of all the things you've reached for where you felt you did your best. Then, make a list of the strengths and qualities you used to accomplish those tasks. Remember to use those strengths and qualities for every creative project. Sophie said, "Reach for the best, for the highest, and for the dreams resting inside you." Place this list in your room where you can read it often. Read it every morning for one week, then see how much stronger you feel inside.

Exercise #8—Chapters 10 and 21

Make a crown of wisdom. If the weather is warm, gather some flowers (clovers, dandelions, etc.) from your yard or a nearby park. Let your mother help you braid them together to make a crown. If the weather is too cold, cut out paper flowers and color them. At the center of each flower, write a wise thought. For example: *I am brave, I am smart*, or *I am happy*. Then, paste them together to make a crown to wear. Whether your crown is made of paper or fresh flowers, you will feel as wise as Sophia, The Goddess of Wisdom, when you wear it.

Exercise #9

Finally, using construction paper cut out more flowers, and list dreams and possibilities on them. So, that you won't forget, tack them on your bulletin board or paste them around your room. Dreams can come true!

Meet the Author/Illustrator

It is an honor and privilege to tell you about my sacred friend, Ilene Satala, who took part of my dream and turned it into a reality. I knew Ilene could paint the illustrations for this book because she is a gifted artist; however, what I did not know was her secret ability to tell a story. After several discussions, my husband, George, and I decided that Goddess Ilene was the one to write Sophia's story.

The two of us spent numerous hours with Ilene expressing what we needed in the book. The story was to build and foster self-esteem, self-worth, and self-acceptance using Sophia and the Seven Goddesses. Ilene took our ideas, combined them with her own creative imagination, and spun an enchanting story that makes a difference for anyone who reads it.

Please allow me to share with you a little about Ilene's artistic abilities. Her paintings are created, not just to be seen, but to be felt. Her work is a 'call' to remember the sacred feminine, Sophia. Her goal is to help people find deeper meaning in their lives through her art.

Ilene's own words: "Since I was a child, I have been entertaining neighborhood children with my stories. I began drawing and painting when I was four years old; however, I find the original thrill of creativity flows brighter the longer I live. I did not know it when I was younger, but wisdom has always been with me, guiding my life's path. Writing this book has allowed me to do my part to help bring back wisdom to the world."

Ilene wrote a wonderful letter describing how she felt about this opportunity to tell Sophia's story. This is what she said: "I wish to thank Beverley and George Danusis for gifting me the project of writing and illustrating this book. Beverley fills me with grace and wisdom, like Sophia herself."

We know that we could not have found anyone to write and illustrate the story better than Goddess Ilene. Thank you from the bottom of our hearts!

—**Goddess Beverley and George Danusis**

Meet the SophiaDolls™
Expanding the Definition of Beauty™

Now that you have read, *Sophia and the Seven Goddesses: A Journey to Self-Acceptance,* it's time to meet the complementary learning tools—SophiaDolls. These dolls expand the definition of beauty by using mythological stories that teach. SophiaDolls act as "Goddess Teachers" through their varied body images, skin tones, and story lessons—which inspire you to be all that you can be. The dolls' diversity demonstrates that beauty comes in all shapes, sizes, and colors.

Everyone is born with innate gifts of wisdom. SophiaDolls divides these gifts into seven unique qualities: creativity, generosity, intuition, centeredness, independence, leadership, and friendship. These inner forces influence our behavior and the way we see, feel, act, and think about others and ourselves. Each SophiaDoll represents ones of these seven innate gifts that may need further development. Just as Sophie and Tena discovered they had innate gifts of wisdom to handle any situation, we can too. We believe that SophiaDolls become the reminders and affirmers of our inner gifts. All SophiaDolls are based in Greek Mythology.

Goddess Athena—Leadership

Athena emerged from her father's head a fully-grown woman clad in golden armor. She stands 16 inches tall, has dark brown hair, perceptive grey eyes, and has a look of confidence on her face. She is dressed in an early Greek costume—a yellow tunic, long skirt, shawl with gold flecks, and a gold vest displaying the head of Medusa. Because she is her father's daughter, we believe we have captured the essence of strength and self-assuredness in the Athena doll. Her story encourages young girls to be leaders and supports "girls being smart." Athena's innate gift is Leadership, which promotes achievement, education, determination, and self-esteem. Athena's body type is based on a small to medium build, size 8. (See more about Athena: *www.sophiadolls.com*)

Goddess Demeter—Generosity

Demeter was the Great Mother Goddess who fed and nurtured the world. She stands 15 3/4 inches tall, has green eyes, harvest-blonde hair, and inviting facial features. She wears a full-length white toga with fluted green edges, which is tied across the bodice with gold braids, and a beautiful green satin-hooded cape. As a caretaker, Demeter's story teaches young girls to love and prepare themselves for the significant time in their lives that is approaching—their menstrual cycle. Her guidance also promotes good eating habits and hygiene. Demeter's story additionally provides clarity for the bond between mother and daughter since she is eternally bonded to her daughter, Goddess Persephone. Demeter's body type is based on a large build, size 16. (See more about Demeter: *www.sophiadolls.com*)

Goddess Persephone—Intuition

Persephone was Demeter's daughter and loved to frolic in the fields picking wild flowers. One day Persephone was captured by the mighty god, Hades, who took her to the Underworld to be his queen. We have captured the innocent, childlike, and playful essence of Goddess Persephone in our doll. She stands 14 1/2 inches tall, has deep violet eyes, strawberry-blonde hair, and a youthful, freckled face. She wears a white toga with indigo-fluted and decorated edges, an indigo over-jacket, and a shawl. Goddess Persephone's personality role was "the daughter" and her story instructs girls to listen to their inner voice. She represents the gift of Intuition and teaches the significance of being open to change and how to transform dreams into reality. Persephone's body type is based on a petite woman's build, size 4-6. (See more about Persephone: *www.sophiadolls.com*)

Goddess Artemis—Independence

Artemis was known as Goddess of the Hunt and the Moon. We have captured the essence of the self-sufficient advocate for women, children, and wild life in our Artemis doll. She stands 17 1/2 inches tall, with soft, black hair, and dark-brown eyes. Her wardrobe consists of a short, cream-colored tunic with red accessories, a belt, buskins, and a bow and arrow quiver that hangs over her shoulder. Artemis epitomizes the personality role of the independent "big sister". Her story educates young girls about being independent, and that having a strong sense of identity is only natural. Artemis, the animal and environment lover teaches respect for nature. She represents the gift of Independence, and teaches girls how to create boundaries with others and that being assertive is a good thing. Artemis' body type is based on a fit, athletic build, size 10. (See more about Artemis: *www.sophiadolls.com*)

Goddess Aphrodite—Creativity

Aphrodite was the most beautiful of the goddesses and was revered as lovely and enchanting. Her essence inspires the arts in every form in our Aphrodite doll. She stands 16 1/2 inches tall, with pale-blond hair and marine-blue eyes. Her attire consists of a cream and orange-layered dress including adornments—a gold tiara, a jeweled cuff bracelet, and earrings. She is everyone's "dazzling aunt" and inspires young girls to appreciate the arts such as music, poetry, dancing, writing, painting, and architectural design. She represents the gift of Creativity and teaches the gift of spontaneity and enthusiasm and how it makes a difference in life. Aphrodite also brings a strong message regarding being comfortable with oneself, especially in one's body, regardless of the shape, size, or height. Her body type is based on a full-figure build, size 14. (See more about Aphrodite: *www.sophiadolls.com*)

Goddess Hestia—Centeredness

Hestia was known as Goddess of the Hearth. She is the peaceful, centered, and pious goddess. She stands 15 inches tall, with burgundy-red hair and calm, lavender eyes. She wears a white toga trimmed with violet-fluted edges, an ornately-decorated shawl, an elegant bracelet, and carries a long torch, which is the Greek perpetual flame symbol. Hestia was the wise woman and represents the personality role grandmother. She schools young girls in values and morals, and the significance of rituals and ceremonies. Hestia represents the gift of Centeredness, and promotes the value of keeping things organized, as well as the importance of respecting elders. Her body type is based on a large frame, size 18. (See more about Hestia: *www.sophiadolls.com*)

Goddess Hera—Friendship

Hera is considered the Queen of Mount Olympus. She has a regal and poised appearance befitting a great lady. She stands 16 3/4 inches tall, has jet-black hair and soulful cobalt-blue eyes. Her symbol, the peacock, is used throughout the designs on her dress, scarf, and sandals. Her apparel consists of a Grecian sky-blue tunic and skirt, and a matching shawl that is trimmed with a dark-green embroidery design. She wears a crown, majestic necklace, gold earrings, and jeweled bracelet. Hera represents the role model of a friend, bride, and *Grande dame*. She represents the gift of Friendship and encourages "girl power" and equality, and teaches girls about abundance and how to be responsible with money and power. Hera shows girls how to constructively change feelings of jealously, anger, and resentment. Her body type is based on a medium regal build, size12. (See more about Hera: *www.sophiadolls.com*)

SophiaDolls were created to communicate powerful images. Our mind often understands symbols more easily and interprets them based on the context in which the object is viewed. Your Sophia doll communicates a strong positive image and will encourage you to use your intuition with other females so that together you can discover how the goddesses' attributes, within your unconscious mind, can be further developed. The entire SophiaDolls collection was designed to connect you with your inner wisdom—or as we prefer to call it, Sophia—to guide, expand, and help bring about balance in your life. Your doll is the liaison between you and your potential. Thinking about one of your SophiaDolls will cause her particular strengths to surface in your conscious awareness. All SophiaDolls represent ancient wisdom.

Eventually, you will want to own each doll and have your own wisdom doll collection. To get started, begin with the doll that has the most attraction for your loved one. Encourage her to use her intuition or use what Sophie taught her in the book about how to make decisions using her heart. Once you've read the book, it is important to reinforce and enhance the experience by introducing a SophiaDoll as the visual reminder of the special gift your loved one represents.

To learn more about SophiaDolls and their mythology, please visit our web site at *www.sophiadolls.com*. You will appreciate our Goddess Quiz, which will help you determine the present leading goddess style in your life. We also encourage you to sign up for our mailing list so you can be kept informed with the latest SophiaDolls news and product offerings. SophiaDolls creator, Beverley Danusis, is an accomplished keynote speaker, author, and workshop leader. *SophiaWoman* Bev brings her mission to life, and inspires you and the girls in your life to live the life of your dreams. Contact her at Bev@sophiadolls.com to schedule a workshop, interview, or speaking engagement.